P9-DHH-186

VENTRESS MEMORIAL LIBRARY (MARSHFIELD)

3 1637 00209 2874

DISCARDED

JUN 13 2007

WASHINGTON IRVING'S

The Legend of
Sleepy Hollow
and Other Stories

Suddenly he heard a groan,—his teeth chattered and his knees smote against the saddle....

WASHINGTON IRVING'S
The Legend of
Sleepy Hollow
and Other Stories

By Washington Irving

Illustrated by Nenad Jakesevic

Ventress Memorial Library
Library Plaza
Marshfield, MA 02050

Illustrated Junior Library®

GROSSET & DUNLAP • PUBLISHERS
NEW YORK

Illustrations copyright © 1999 by Nenad Jakesevic. All rights reserved. Published by
Grosset & Dunlap, a division of Penguin Putnam Books for Young Readers,
New York. Published simultaneously in Canada. Printed in the United States of
America. *Illustrated Junior Library* is a registered trademark of Grosset & Dunlap, Inc.

Library of Congress Cataloging-in-Publication Data

Irving, Washington, 1783-1859.
    Washington Irving's The legend of Sleepy Hollow and other stories / by Washington
Irving ; illustrated by Nenad Jakesevic.
        p. cm. -- (Illustrated junior library)
    Summary: A collection of stories by Washington Irving, including "Rip Van Winkle,"
"The Spectre of Bridegroom," and "The Bold Dragoon."
    1. Children's stories, American. [1. Short stories.]
I. Jakesevic, Nenad, ill. II. Title. III. Title: Legend of Sleepy Hollow and other Stories.
IV. Series
PZ7.I68Was   1999
[Fic]--dc21   99-36264
                                                                                                           CIP

ISBN 0-448-42074-0   2007 Printing

Contents

The Legend of Sleepy Hollow

Found Among the Papers of the Late
Diedrich Knickerbocker

A pleasing land of drowsy head it was,
Of dreams that wave before the half-shut eye,
And of gay castles in the clouds that pass,
For ever flushing round the summer sky.
                                    Castle of Indolence.

In the bosom of one of those spacious coves which indent the eastern shore of the Hudson, at the broad expansion of the river denominated by the ancient Dutch navigators the Tappan Zee, and where they always prudently shortened sail, and implored the protection of St. Nicholas when they crossed, there lies a small market-town or rural port, which by some is called Greensburgh, but which is more generally and properly known by the name of Tarry Town. This name was given, we are told, in former days, by the good housewives of the adjacent country, from the inveterate propensity of their husbands to linger about the village tavern on market-days. Be that as it may, I do not vouch for the fact, but merely advert to it for the sake of being precise and authentic. Not far from this village, perhaps about two miles, there is a little valley, or rather lap of land, among high hills, which is one of the quietest places in the whole world. A small brook glides through it, with just murmur enough to lull one to repose; and the occasional whistle of a quail, or tapping of a woodpecker, is almost the only sound that ever breaks in upon the uniform tranquillity.

I recollect that, when a stripling, my first exploit in squirrel-shooting was in a grove of tall walnut-trees that shades one side of the valley. I had wandered into it at noon-time, when all nature is particularly quiet, and was startled by the roar of my own gun, as it broke the Sabbath stillness around, and was prolonged and reverberated by the angry echoes. If ever I should wish for a retreat, whither I might steal from the world and its distractions, and dream quietly away the remnant of a troubled life, I know of none more promising than this little valley.

From the listless repose of the place, and the peculiar character of its inhabitants, who are descendants from the original Dutch settlers, this sequestered glen has long been known by the name of SLEEPY HOLLOW, and its rustic lads are called the Sleepy Hollow Boys throughout all the neighboring country. A drowsy, dreamy influence seems to hang over the land, and to pervade the very atmosphere. Some say that the place was bewitched by a high German doctor, during the early days of the settlement; others, that an old Indian chief, the prophet or wizard of his tribe, held his pow-wows there before the country was discovered by Master Hendrick Hudson. Certain it is, the place still continues under the sway of some bewitching power, that holds a spell over the minds of the good people, causing them to walk in a continual reverie. They are given to all kinds of marvellous beliefs; are subject to trances and visions; and frequently see strange sights, and hear music and voices in the air. The whole neighborhood abounds with local tales, haunted spots, and twilight superstitions; stars shoot and meteors glare oftener across the valley than in any other part of the country, and the nightmare, with her whole ninefold, seems to make it the favorite scene of her gambols.

The dominant spirit, however, that haunts this enchanted region, and seems to be commander-in-chief of all the powers of the air, is the apparition of a figure on horseback without a head. It is said by some to be the ghost of a Hessian trooper, whose head had been carried away by a cannon-ball, in some nameless battle during the Revolutionary War, and who is ever and anon seen by the country folk, hurrying along in the gloom of night, as if on the wings of the wind. His haunts are not confined to the valley, but extend at times to the adjacent roads, and especially to the vicinity of a church at no great distance. Indeed, certain of the most authentic historians of those parts, who have been careful in collecting and collating the floating facts concerning this spectre, allege that the body of the trooper having been buried in the churchyard, the ghost rides forth to the scene of battle in nightly quest of his head; and that the rushing speed with which he sometimes passes along the Hollow, like a midnight blast, is owing to his being belated, and in a hurry to get back to the churchyard before daybreak.

Such is the general purport of this legendary superstition, which has furnished materials for many a wild story in that region of shadows; and the spectre is known, at all the country firesides, by the name of the Headless Horseman of Sleepy Hollow.

It is remarkable that the visionary propensity I have mentioned is not confined to the native inhabitants of the valley, but is unconsciously imbibed by every one who resides there for a time. However wide awake they may have been before they entered that sleepy region, they are sure, in a little time, to inhale the witching influence of the air, and begin to grow imaginative, to dream dreams, and see apparitions.

I mention this peaceful spot with all possible laud; for it is in such little retired Dutch valleys, found here and there embosomed in the great State of New York, that population, manners, and customs remain fixed; while the great torrent of migration and improvement, which is making such incessant changes in other parts of this restless country, sweeps by them unobserved. They are like those little nooks of still water which border a rapid stream; where we may see the straw and bubble riding quietly at anchor, or slowly revolving in their mimic harbor, undisturbed by the rush of the passing current. Though many years have elapsed since I trod the drowsy shades of Sleepy Hollow, yet I question whether I should not still find the same trees and the same families vegetating in its sheltered bosom.

In this by-place of nature, there abode, in a remote period of American history, that is to say, some thirty years since, a worthy wight of the name of Ichabod Crane; who sojourned, or, as he expressed it, "tarried," in Sleepy Hollow, for the purpose of instructing the children of the vicinity. He was a native of Connecticut, a State which supplies the Union with pioneers for the mind as well as for the forest, and sends forth yearly its legions of frontier woodsmen and country schoolmasters. The cognomen of Crane was not inapplicable to his person. He was tall, but exceedingly lank, with narrow shoulders, long arms and legs, hands that dangled a mile out of his sleeves, feet that might have served for shovels, and his whole frame most loosely hung together. His head was small, and flat at top, with huge ears, large green glassy eyes, and a long snipe nose, so that it looked like a weathercock perched upon his spindle neck, to tell which way the wind blew. To see him striding along the profile of a hill on a windy day, with his clothes bagging and fluttering about him, one might have mistaken him for the genius of famine descending upon the earth, or some scarecrow eloped from a corn-field.

His school-house was a low building of one large room, rudely constructed of logs; the windows partly glazed, and partly patched with leaves of old copy-books. It was most ingeniously secured at vacant hours by a withe twisted in the handle of the door, and stakes set against the window-shutters; so that, though a thief might get in with perfect ease, he would find some embarrassment in getting out: an idea most probably borrowed by the architect, Yost Van Houten, from the mystery of an eel-pot. The school-house stood in a rather lonely but pleasant situation, just at the foot of a woody hill, with a brook running close by, and a formidable birch-tree growing at one end of it. From hence the low murmur of his pupils' voices, conning over their lessons, might be heard on a drowsy summer's day, like the hum of a bee-hive; interrupted now and then by the authoritative voice of the master, in the tone of menace or command; or, peradventure, by the appalling sound of the birch, as he urged some tardy loiterer along the flowery path of knowledge. Truth to say, he was a conscientious man, and ever bore in mind the golden maxim, "Spare the rod and spoil the child."—Ichabod Crane's scholars certainly were not spoiled.

I would not have it imagined, however, that he was one of those cruel potentates of the school, who joy in the smart of their subjects; on the contrary, he administered justice with discrimination rather than severity, taking the burden off the backs of the weak, and laying it on those of the strong. Your mere puny stripling, that winced at the least flourish of the rod, was passed by with indulgence; but the claims of justice were satisfied by inflicting a double portion on some little, tough, wrong-headed, broad-skirted Dutch urchin, who sulked and swelled and grew dogged and sullen beneath the birch. All this he called "doing his duty" by their parents; and he never inflicted a chastisement without following it by the assurance, so consolatory to the smarting urchin, that "he would remember it, and thank him for it the longest day he had to live."

When school-hours were over, he was even the compan-

ion and playmate of the larger boys; and on holiday after-
noons would convoy some of the smaller ones home, who
happened to have pretty sisters, or good housewives for
mothers, noted for the comforts of the cupboard. Indeed it
behooved him to keep on good terms with his pupils. The
revenue arising from his school was small, and would have
been scarcely sufficient to furnish him with daily bread, for
he was a huge feeder, and, though lank, had the dilating
powers of an anaconda; but to help out his maintenance, he
was, according to country custom in those parts, boarded
and lodged at the houses of the farmers, whose children he
instructed. With these he lived successively a week at a time;
thus going the rounds of the neighborhood, with all his
worldly effects tied up in a cotton handkerchief.

That all this might not be too onerous on the purses of his
rustic patrons, who are apt to consider the costs of schooling
a grievous burden, and schoolmasters as mere drones, he
had various ways of rendering himself both useful and
agreeable. He assisted the farmers occasionally in the lighter
labors of their farms; helped to make hay; mended the fences;
took the horses to water; drove the cows from pasture; and
cut wood for the winter fire. He laid aside, too, all the dominant dignity and absolute sway with which he lorded it in his
little empire, the school, and became wonderfully gentle and
ingratiating. He found favor in the eyes of the mothers, by
petting the children, particularly the youngest; and like the
lion bold, which whilom so magnanimously the lamb did
hold, he would sit with a child on one knee, and rock a cra-
dle with his foot for whole hours together.

In addition to his other vocations, he was the singing-master of the neighborhood, and picked up many bright shillings by instructing the young folks in psalmody. It was a matter of no little vanity to him, on Sundays, to take his station in front of the church-gallery, with a band of chosen singers; where, in his own mind, he completely carried away the psalm from the parson. Certain it is, his voice resounded far above all the rest of the congregation; and there are peculiar quavers still to be heard in that church, and which may even be heard half a mile off, quite to the opposite side of the mill-pond, on a still Sunday morning, which are said to be legitimately descended from the nose of Ichabod Crane. Thus, by divers little makeshifts in that ingenious way which is commonly denominated "by hook and by crook," the worthy pedagogue got on tolerably enough, and was thought, by all who understood nothing of the labor of headwork, to have a wonderfully easy life of it.

The schoolmaster is generally a man of some importance in the female circle of a rural neighborhood; being considered a kind of idle, gentleman-like personage, of vastly superior taste and accomplishments to the rough country swains, and, indeed, inferior in learning only to the parson. His appearance, therefore, is apt to occasion some little stir at the tea-table of a farm-house, and the addition of a supernumerary dish of cakes or sweet-meats, or, peradventure, the parade of a silver tea-pot. Our man of letters, therefore, was peculiarly happy in the smiles of all the country damsels. How he would figure among them in the churchyard, between services on Sundays! gathering grapes for them from the wild vines that overrun the surrounding trees; reciting for their amusement all the epitaphs on the tombstones; or saunter-ing, with a whole bevy of them, along the banks of the adja-cent mill-pond; while the more bashful country bumpkins hung sheepishly back, envying his superior elegance and address.

From his half itinerant life, also, he was a kind of travel-ling gazette, carrying the whole budget of local gossip from house to house: so that his appearance was always greeted with satisfaction. He was, moreover, esteemed by the women as a man of great erudition, for he had read several books quite through, and was a perfect master of Cotton Mather's *History of New England Witchcraft*, in which, by the way, he most firmly and potently believed.

He was, in fact, an odd mixture of small shrewdness and simple credulity. His appetite for the marvellous, and his powers of digesting it, were equally extraordinary; and both had been increased by his residence in this spellbound region. No tale was too gross or monstrous for his capacious swallow. It was often his delight, after his school was dis-missed in the afternoon, to stretch himself on the rich bed of clover bordering the little brook that whimpered by his school-house, and there con over old Mather's direful tales, until the gathering dusk of the evening made the printed page a mere mist before his eyes. Then, as he wended his way, by swamp and stream, and awful woodland, to the farm-house where he happened to be quartered, every sound of nature, at that witching hour, fluttered his excited imagi-nation; the moan of the whippoorwill from the hill-side, the boding cry of the treetoad, that harbinger of storm; the dreary hooting of the screech-owl, or the sudden rustling in the thicket of birds frightened from their roost. The fire-flies, too, which sparkled most vividly in the darkest places, now and then startled him, as one of uncommon brightness would stream across his path; and if, by chance, a huge blockhead of a beetle came winging his blundering flight against him, the poor varlet was ready to give up the ghost, with the idea that he was struck with a witch's token. His only resource on such occasions, either to drown thought or drive away evil spirits, was to sing psalm-tunes; and the good people of Sleepy Hollow, as they sat by their doors of an evening, were often filled with awe, at hearing his nasal melody, "in linked sweetness long drawn out," floating from the distant hill, or along the dusky road.

Another of his sources of fearful pleasure was, to pass long winter evenings with the old Dutch wives, as they sat spinning by the fire, with a row of apples roasting and spluttering along the hearth, and listen to their marvellous tales of ghosts and goblins, and haunted fields, and haunted brooks, and haunted bridges, and haunted houses, and particularly of the headless horseman, or Galloping Hessian of the Hollow, as they sometimes called him. He would delight them equally by his anecdotes of witchcraft, and the direful omens and portentous sights and sounds in the air, which prevailed in the earlier times of Connecticut; and would frighten them woefully with speculations upon comets and shooting-stars, and with the alarming fact that the world did absolutely turn round, and that they were half the time topsy-turvy!

But if there was a pleasure in all this, while snugly cuddling in the chimney-corner of a chamber that was all of a ruddy glow from the crackling wood-fire, and where, of course, no spectre dared to show his face, it was dearly purchased by the terrors of his subsequent walk homewards. What fearful shapes and shadows beset his path amidst the dim and ghastly glare of a snowy night!—With what wistful look did he eye every trembling ray of light streaming across the waste fields from some distant window!—How often was he appalled by some shrub covered with snow, which, like a sheeted spectre, beset his very path!—How often did he shrink with curdling awe at the sound of his own steps on a frosty crust beneath his feet; and dread to look over his shoulder, lest he should behold some uncouth being tramping close behind him!—and how often was he thrown into complete dismay by some rushing blast, howling among the trees, in the idea that it was the Galloping Hessian on one of his nightly scourings!

All these, however, were mere terrors of the night, phantoms of the mind that walk in darkness; and though he had seen many spectres in his time, and been more than once beset by Satan in divers shapes, in his lonely perambulations, yet daylight put an end to all these evils; and he would have passed a pleasant life of it, in despite of the devil and all his works, if his path had not been crossed by a being that causes more perplexity to mortal man than ghosts, goblins, and the whole race of witches put together, and that was—a woman.

Among the musical disciples who assembled, one evening in each week, to receive his instructions in psalmody, was Katrina Van Tassel, the daughter and only child of a substantial Dutch farmer. She was a blooming lass of fresh eighteen; plump as a partridge; ripe and melting and rosy-cheeked as one of her father's peaches, and universally famed, not merely for her beauty, but her vast expectations. She was withal a little of a coquette, as might be perceived even in her dress, which was a mixture of ancient and modern fashions, as most suited to set off her charms. She wore the ornaments of pure yellow gold, which her great-great-grandmother had brought over from Saardam; the tempting stomacher of the olden time; and withal a provokingly short petticoat, to display the prettiest foot and ankle in the country round.

Ichabod Crane had a soft and foolish heart towards the sex; and it is not to be wondered at that so tempting a morsel soon found favor in his eyes; more especially after he had visited her in her paternal mansion. Old Baltus Van Tassel was a perfect picture of a thriving, contented, liberal-hearted farmer. He seldom, it is true, sent his eyes or his thoughts beyond the boundaries of his own farm; but within those everything was snug, happy, and well-conditioned. He was satisfied with his wealth, but not proud of it; and piqued himself upon the hearty abundance rather than the style in which he lived. His stronghold was situated on the banks of the Hudson, in one of those green, sheltered, fertile nooks in which the Dutch farmers are so fond of nestling. A great elm-tree spread its broad branches over it; at the foot of which bubbled up a spring of the softest and sweetest water, in a little well, formed of a barrel; and then stole sparkling away through the grass, to a neighboring brook, that bubbled along among alders and dwarf willows. Hard by the farm-house was a vast barn, that might have served for a church; every window and crevice of which seemed bursting forth with the treasures of the farm; the flail was busily resounding within it from morning till night; swallows and martins skimmed twittering about the eaves; and rows of pigeons, some with one eye turned up, as if watching the weather, some with their heads under their wings, or buried in their bosoms, and others swelling, and cooing, and bowing about their dames, were enjoying the sunshine on the roof. Sleek unwieldy porkers were grunting in the repose and abundance of their pens; whence sallied forth, now and then, troops of sucking pigs, as if to snuff the air. A stately squadron of snowy geese were riding in an adjoining pond, convoying whole fleets of ducks; regiments of turkeys were gobbling through the farm-yard, and guinea fowls fretting about it, like ill-tempered housewives, with their peevish discontented cry. Before the barn-door strutted the gallant cock, that pattern of a husband, a warrior, and a fine gentleman, clapping his burnished wings, and crowing in the pride and gladness of his heart–sometimes tearing up the earth with his feet, and then generously calling his ever-hungry family of wives and children to enjoy the rich morsel which he had discovered.

The pedagogue's mouth watered, as he looked upon this sumptuous promise of luxurious winter fare. In his devouring mind's eye he pictured to himself every roasting-pig running about with a pudding in his belly, and an apple in his mouth; the pigeons were snugly put to bed in a comfortable pie, and tucked in with a coverlet of crust; the geese were swimming in their own gravy; and the ducks pairing cosily in dishes, like snug married couples, with a decent competency of onion-sauce. In the porkers he saw carved out the future sleek side of bacon, and juicy relishing ham; not a turkey but he beheld daintily trussed up, with its gizzard under its wing, and, peradventure, a necklace of savory sausages; and even bright chanticleer himself lay sprawling on his back, in a side-dish, with uplifted claws, as if craving that quarter which his chivalrous spirit disdained to ask while living.

As the enraptured Ichabod fancied all this, and as he rolled his great green eyes over the fat meadow-lands, the rich fields of wheat, of rye, of buckwheat, and Indian corn, and the orchard burdened with ruddy fruit, which surrounded the warm tenement of Van Tassel, his heart yearned after the damsel who was to inherit these domains, and his imagination expanded with the idea how they might be readily turned into cash, and the money invested in immense tracts of wild land, and shingle palaces in the wilderness. Nay, his busy fancy already realized his hopes, and presented to him the blooming Katrina, with a whole family of children, mounted on the top of a wagon loaded with household trumpery, with pots and kettles dangling beneath; and he beheld himself bestriding a pacing mare, with a colt at her heels, setting out for Kentucky, Tennessee, or the Lord knows where.

When he entered the house, the conquest of his heart was complete. It was one of those spacious farm-houses, with high-ridged, but lowly-sloping roofs, built in the style handed down from the first Dutch settlers; the low projecting eaves forming a piazza along the front, capable of being closed up in bad weather. Under this were hung flails, harness, various utensils of husbandry, and nets for fishing in the neighboring river. Benches were built along the sides for summer use; and a great spinning-wheel at one end, and a churn at the other, showed the various uses to which this important porch might be devoted. From this piazza the wandering Ichabod entered the hall, which formed the centre of the mansion and the place of usual residence. Here, rows of resplendent pewter, ranged on a long dresser, dazzled his eyes. In one corner stood a huge bag of wool ready to be spun; in another a quantity of linsey-woolsey just from the loom; ears of Indian corn, and strings of dried apples and peaches, hung in gay festoons along the walls, mingled with the gaud of red peppers; and a door left ajar gave him a peep into the best parlor, where the claw-footed chairs and dark mahogany tables shone like mirrors; and irons, with their accompanying shovel and tongs, glistened from their covert of asparagus tops; mock-oranges and conch-shells decorated the mantel-piece; strings of various colored birds' eggs were suspended above it, a great ostrich egg was hung from the centre of the room, and a corner-cupboard, knowingly left open, displayed immense treasures of old silver and well-mended china.

From the moment Ichabod laid his eyes upon these regions of delight, the peace of his mind was at an end, and his only study was how to gain the affections of the peerless daughter of Van Tassel. In this enterprise, however, he had more real difficulties than generally fell to the lot of a knight-errant of yore, who seldom had anything but giants, enchanters, fiery dragons, and such like easily conquered adversaries, to contend with; and had to make his way merely through gates of iron and brass, and walls of adamant, to the castle-keep, where the lady of his heart was confined; all which he achieved as easily as a man would carve his way to the centre of a Christmas pie; and then the lady gave him her hand as a matter of course. Ichabod, on the contrary, had to win his way to the heart of a country coquette, beset with a labyrinth of whims and caprices, which were forever presenting new difficulties and impediments; and he had to encounter a host of fearful adversaries of real flesh and blood, the numerous rustic admirers, who beset every portal to her heart; keeping a watchful and angry eye upon each other, but ready to fly out in the common cause against any new competitor.

Among these the most formidable was a burly, roaring, roistering blade, of the name of Abraham, or, according to the Dutch abbreviation, Brom Van Brunt, the hero of the country round, which rang with his feats of strength and hardihood. He was broad-shouldered and double-jointed, with short, curly black hair, and a bluff but not unpleasant countenance, having a mingled air of fun and arrogance. From his Herculean frame and great powers of limb, he had received the nickname of BROM BONES, by which he was universally known. He was famed for great knowledge and skill in horsemanship, being as dexterous on horseback as a Tartar. He was foremost at all races and cockfights; and, with the ascendancy which bodily strength acquires in rustic life, was the umpire in all disputes, setting his hat on one side, and giving his decisions with an air and tone admitting of no gainsay or appeal. He was always ready for either a fight or a frolic; but had more mischief than ill-will in his composition; and, with all his overbearing roughness, there was a strong dash of waggish good-humor at the bottom. He had three or four boon companions, who regarded him as their model, and at the head of whom he scoured the country, attending every scene of feud or merriment for miles round. In cold weather he was distinguished by a fur cap, surmounted with a flaunting fox's tail; and when the folks at a country gathering descried this well-known crest at a distance, whisking about among a squad of hard riders, they always stood by for a squall. Sometimes his crew would be heard dashing along past the farm-houses at midnight, with whoop and halloo, like a troop of Don Cossacks; and the old dames, startled out of their sleep, would listen for a moment till the hurry-scurry had clattered by, and then exclaim, "Ay, there goes Brom Bones and his gang!" The neighbors looked upon him with a mixture of awe, admiration, and good-will;

and when any madcap prank, or rustic brawl, occurred in the vicinity, always shook their heads, and warranted Brom Bones was at the bottom of it.

This rantipole hero had for some time singled out the blooming Katrina for the object of his uncouth gallantries; and though his amorous toyings were something like the gentle caresses and endearments of a bear, yet it was whispered that she did not altogether discourage his hopes. Certain it is, his advances were signals for rival candidates to retire, who felt no inclination to cross a line in his amours; insomuch, that, when his horse was seen tied to Van Tassel's paling on a Sunday night, a sure sign that his master was courting, or, as it is termed, "sparking," within, all other suitors passed by in despair, and carried the war into other quarters.

Such was the formidable rival with whom Ichabod Crane had to contend, and, considering all things, a stouter man than he would have shrunk from the competition, and a wiser man would have despaired. He had, however, a happy mixture of pliability and perseverance in his nature; he was in form and spirit like a supple-jack—yielding, but tough; though he bent, he never broke; and though he bowed beneath the slightest pressure yet, the moment it was away—jerk! he was as erect, and carried his head as high as ever.

To have taken the field openly against his rival would have been madness; for he was not a man to be thwarted in his amours, any more than that stormy lover, Achilles. Ichabod, therefore, made his advances in a quiet and gently insinuating manner. Under cover of his character of singing-master, he had made frequent visits at the farmhouse; not that he had anything to apprehend from the meddlesome interference of parents, which is so often a stumbling-block in the path of lovers. Balt Van Tassel was an easy, indulgent soul; he loved his daughter better even than his pipe, and, like a reasonable man and an excellent father, let her have her way in everything. His notable little wife, too, had enough to do to attend to her housekeeping and manage her poultry; for, as she sagely observed, ducks and geese are foolish things, and must be looked after, but girls can take care of themselves. Thus while the busy dame bustled about the house, or plied her spinning-wheel at one end of the piazza, honest Balt would sit smoking his evening pipe at the other, watching the achievements of a little wooden warrior, who, armed with a sword in each hand, was most valiantly fighting the wind on the pinnacle of the barn. In the meantime, Ichabod would carry on his suit with the daughter by the side of the spring under the great elm, or sauntering along in the twilight,—that hour so favorable to the lover's eloquence.

I profess not to know how women's hearts are wooed and won. To me they have always been matters of riddle and admiration. Some seem to have but one vulnerable point or door of access, while others have a thousand avenues, and may be captured in a thousand different ways. It is a great triumph of skill to gain the former, but a still greater proof of generalship to maintain possession of the latter, for the man must battle for his fortress at every door and window. He who wins a thousand common hearts is therefore entitled to some renown; but he who keeps undisputed sway over the heart of a coquette, is indeed a hero. Certain it is, this was not the case with the redoubtable Brom Bones; and from the moment Ichabod Crane made his advances, the interests of the former evidently declined; his horse was no longer seen tied at the palings on Sunday nights, and a deadly feud gradually arose between him and the preceptor of Sleepy Hollow.

Brom, who had a degree of rough chivalry in his nature, would fain have carried matters to open warfare, and have settled their pretensions to the lady according to the mode of those most concise and simple reasoners, the knights-errant of yore–by single combat; but Ichabod was too conscious of the superior might of his adversary to enter the lists against him: he had overheard a boast of Bones, that he would "double the schoolmaster up, and lay him on a shelf of his own schoolhouse;" and he was too wary to give him an opportunity. There was something extremely provoking in this obstinately pacific system; it left Brom no alternative but to draw upon the funds of rustic waggery in his disposition, and to play off boorish practical jokes upon his rival. Ichabod became the object of whimsical persecution to Bones and his gang of rough riders. They harried his hitherto peaceful domains; smoked out his singing-school, by stopping up the chimney; broke into the school-house at night, in spite of its formidable fastenings of withe and window-stakes, and turned everything topsy-turvy; so that the poor schoolmaster began to think all the witches in the country held their meetings there. But what was still more annoying, Brom took opportunities of turning him into ridicule in presence of his mistress, and had a scoundrel dog whom he taught to whine in the most ludicrous manner, and introduced as a rival of Ichabod's to instruct her in psalmody.

In this way matters went on for some time, without producing any material effect on the relative situation of the contending powers. On a fine autumnal afternoon, Ichabod, in a pensive mood, sat enthroned on the lofty stool whence he usually watched all the concerns of his little literary realm. In his hand he swayed a ferule, that sceptre of despotic power; the birch of justice reposed on three nails, behind the throne, a constant terror to evil-doers; while on the desk before him might be seen sundry contraband articles and prohibited weapons, detected upon the persons of idle urchins; such as half-munched apples, pop-guns, whirligigs, fly-cages, and whole legions of rampant little paper game-cocks. Apparently there had been some appalling act of justice recently inflicted, for his scholars were all busily intent upon their books, or slyly whispering behind them with one eye kept upon the master; and a kind of buzzing stillness reigned throughout the school-room. It was suddenly interrupted by the appearance of a man, in tow-cloth jacket and trousers, a round-crowned fragment of a hat, like the cap of Mercury, and mounted on the back of a ragged, wild, half-broken colt, which he managed with a rope by way of halter. He came clattering up to the school-door with an invitation to Ichabod to attend a merry-making or "quilting frolic," to be held that evening at Mynheer Van Tassel's. Then he dashed over the brook, and was seen scampering away up the Hollow, full of the importance and hurry of his mission.

All was now bustle and hubbub in the late quiet school-room. The scholars were hurried through their lessons, without stopping at trifles; those who were nimble skipped over half with impunity, and those who were tardy had a smart application now and then in the rear, to quicken their speed, or help them over a tall word. Books were flung aside without being put away on the shelves, inkstands were overturned, benches thrown down, and the whole school was turned loose an hour before the usual time, bursting forth like a legion of young imps, yelping and racketing about the green, in joy at their early emancipation.

The gallant Ichabod now spent at least an extra half-hour at his toilet, brushing and furbishing up his best and indeed only suit of rusty black, and arranging his locks by a bit of broken looking-glass, that hung up in the school-house. That he might make his appearance before his mistress in the true style of a cavalier, he borrowed a horse from the farmer with whom he was domiciliated, a choleric old Dutchman, of the name of Hans Van Ripper, and, thus gallantly mounted, issued forth, like a knight-errant in quest of adventures. But it is meet I should, in the true spirit of romantic story, give some account of the looks and equipments of my hero and his steed. The animal he bestrode was a broken-down plough-horse, that had outlived almost everything but his viciousness. He was gaunt and shagged, with a ewe neck and a head like a hammer; his rusty mane and tail were tangled and knotted with burrs; one eye had lost its pupil, and was glaring and spectral; but the other had the gleam of a genuine devil in it. Still he must have had fire and mettle in his day, if we may judge from the name he bore of Gunpowder. He had, in fact, been a favorite steed of his master's, the choleric Van Ripper, who was a furious rider, and had infused, very probably, some of his own spirit into the animal; for, old and broken-down as he looked, there was more of the lurking devil in him than in any young filly in the country.

Ichabod was a suitable figure for such a steed. He rode with short stirrups, which brought his knees nearly up to the pommel of the saddle; his sharp elbows stuck out like grasshoppers'; he carried his whip perpendicularly in his hand, like a sceptre, and, as his horse jogged on, the motion of his arms was not unlike the flapping of a pair of wings. A small wool hat rested on the top of his nose, for so his scanty strip of forehead might be called; and the skirts of his black coat fluttered out almost to the horse's tail. Such was the appearance of Ichabod and his steed, as they shambled out of the gate of Hans Van Ripper, and it was altogether such an apparition as is seldom to be met with in broad daylight.

It was, as I have said, a fine autumnal day, the sky was clear and nature wore that rich and golden livery which we always associate with the idea of abundance. The forests had put on their sober brown and yellow, while some trees of the tenderer kind had been nipped by the frosts into brilliant dyes of orange, purple, and scarlet. Streaming files of wild ducks began to make their appearance high in the air; the bark of the squirrel might be heard from the groves of beech and hickory nuts, and the pensive whistle of the quail at intervals from the neighboring stubble-field.

The small birds were taking their farewell banquets. In

the fulness of their revelry, they fluttered, chirping and frolicking, from bush to bush, and tree to tree, capricious from the very profusion and variety around them. There was the honest cockrobin, the favorite game of stripling sportsmen, with its loud querulous notes; and the twittering blackbirds flying in sable clouds; and the golden-winged woodpecker, with his crimson crest, his broad black gorget, and splendid plumage; and the cedar-bird, with its red-tipt wings and yellow-tipt tail, and its little monteiro cap of feathers; and the blue jay, that noisy coxcomb, in his gay light-blue coat and white under-clothes, screaming and chattering, nodding and bobbing and bowing, and pretending to be on good terms with every songster of the grove.

As Ichabod jogged slowly on his way, his eye, ever open to every symptom of culinary abundance, ranged with delight over the treasures of jolly autumn. On all sides he beheld vast store of apples; some hanging in oppressive opulence on the trees; some gathered into baskets and barrels for the market; others heaped up in rich piles for the cider-press. Farther on he beheld great fields of Indian corn, with its golden ears peeping from their leafy coverts, and holding out the promise of cakes and hasty-pudding; and the yellow pumpkins lying beneath them, turning up their fair round bellies to the sun, and giving ample prospects of the most luxurious of pies; and anon he passed the fragrant buckwheat fields, breathing the odor of the bee-hive, and as he beheld them, soft anticipations stole over his mind of dainty slapjacks, well buttered, and garnished with honey or treacle, by the delicate little dimpled hand of Katrina Van Tassel.

Thus feeding his mind with many sweet thoughts and "sugared suppositions," he journeyed along the sides of a range of hills which look out upon some of the goodliest scenes of the mighty Hudson. The sun gradually wheeled his broad disk down into the west. The wide bosom of the Tappan Zee lay motionless and glossy, excepting that here and there a gentle undulation waved and prolonged the blue shadow of the distant mountain. A few amber clouds floated in the sky, without a breath of air to move them. The horizon was of a fine golden tint, changing gradually into a pure apple-green, and from that into the deep blue of the mid-heaven. A slanting ray lingered on the woody crests of the precipices that overhung some parts of the river, giving greater depth to the dark-gray and purple of their rocky sides. A sloop was loitering in the distance, dropping slowly down with the tide, her sail hanging uselessly against the mast; and as the reflection of the sky gleamed along the still water, it seemed as if the vessel was suspended in the air.

It was toward evening that Ichabod arrived at the castle of the Heer Van Tassel, which he found thronged with the pride and flower of the adjacent country. Old farmers, a spare leathern-faced race, in homespun coats and breeches, blue stocking, huge shoes, and magnificent pewter buckles. Their brisk withered little dames, in close crimped caps, long-waisted shortgowns, homespun petticoats, with scissors and pincushions, and gay calico pockets hanging on the outside. Buxom lasses, almost as antiquated as their mothers, excepting where a straw hat, a fine ribbon, or perhaps a white frock, gave symptoms of city innovation. The sons, in short square-skirted coats with rows of stupendous brass buttons, and their hair generally queued in the fashion of the times, especially if they could procure an eel-skin for the purpose, it being esteemed, throughout the country, as a potent nourisher and strengthener of the hair.

Brom Bones, however, was the hero of the scene, having come to the gathering on his favorite steed, Daredevil, a creature, like himself, full of mettle and mischief, and which no one but himself could manage. He was, in fact, noted for preferring vicious animals, given to all kinds of tricks, which kept the rider in constant risk of his neck, for he held a tractable well-broken horse as unworthy of a lad of spirit.

Fain would I pause to dwell upon the world of charms that burst upon the enraptured gaze of my hero, as he entered the state parlor of Van Tassel's mansion. Not those of the bevy of buxom lasses, with their luxurious display of red and white; but the ample charms of a genuine Dutch country tea-table, in the sumptuous time of autumn. Such heaped-up platters of cakes of various and almost indescribable kinds, known only to experienced Dutch housewives! There was the doughty doughnut, the tenderer oly koek, and the crisp and crumbling cruller; sweet cakes and short cakes, ginger-cakes and honey-cakes, and the whole family of cakes. And then there were apple-pies and peach-pies and pumpkin-pies; besides slices of ham and smoked beef; and moreover delectable dishes of preserved plums, and peaches, and pears, and quinces; not to mention broiled shad and roasted chickens; together with bowls of milk and cream, all mingled higgledy-piggledy, pretty much as I have enumerated them, with the motherly tea-pot sending up its clouds of vapor from the midst—Heaven bless the mark! I want breath and time to discuss this banquet as it deserves, and am too eager to get on with my story. Happily, Ichabod Crane was not in so great a hurry as his historian, but did ample justice to every dainty.

He was a kind and thankful creature, whose heart dilated in proportion as his skin was filled with good cheer; and whose spirits rose with eating as some men's do with drink. He could not help, too, rolling his large eyes round him as he ate, and chuckling with the possibility that he might one day be lord of all this scene of almost unimaginable luxury and splendor. Then, he thought, how soon he'd turn his back upon the old school-house; snap his fingers in the face of Hans Van Ripper, and every other niggardly patron, and kick any itinerant pedagogue out-of-doors that should dare to call him comrade!

Old Baltus Van Tassel moved about among his guests with a face dilated with content and good-humor, round and jolly as the harvest-moon. His hospitable attentions were brief, but expressive, being confined to a shake of the hand, a slap on the shoulder, a loud laugh, and a pressing invitation to "fall to, and help themselves."

And now the sound of the music from the common room, or hall, summoned to the dance. The musician was an old gray-headed man, who had been the itinerant orchestra of the neighborhood for more than half a century. His instrument was as old and battered as himself. The greater part of the time he scraped on two or three strings, accompanying every movement of the bow with a motion of the head; bowing almost to the ground, and stamping with his foot whenever a fresh couple were to start.

Ichabod prided himself upon his dancing as much as upon his vocal powers. Not a limb, not a fibre about him was idle; and to have seen his loosely hung frame in full motion, and clattering about the room, you would have thought Saint Vitus himself, that blessed patron of the dance, was figuring before you in person. How could the flogger of urchins be otherwise than animated and joyous? The lady of his heart was his partner in the dance, and smiling graciously in reply to all his amorous oglings; while Brom Bones, sorely smitten with love and jealousy, sat brooding by himself in one corner.

When the dance was at an end, Ichabod was attracted to a knot of the sager folks, who, with old Van Tassel, sat smoking at one end of the piazza, gossiping over former times, and drawing out long stories about the war.

This neighborhood, at the time of which I am speaking, was one of those highly favored places which abound with chronicle and great men. The British and American line had run near it during the war; it had, therefore, been the scene of marauding, and infested with refugees, cow-boys, and all kinds of border chivalry. Just sufficient time has elapsed to enable each story-teller to dress up his tale with a little becoming fiction, and, in the indistinctness of his recollection, to make himself the hero of every exploit.

There was the story of Doffue Martling, a large blue-bearded Dutchman, who had nearly taken a British frigate with an old iron ninepounder from a mud breastwork, only that his gun burst at the sixth discharge. And there was an old gentleman who shall be nameless, being too rich a mynheer to be lightly mentioned, who, in the battle of White Plains, being an excellent master of defense, parried a musketball with a small sword, insomuch that he absolutely felt it whiz round the blade, and glance off at the hilt; in proof of which he was ready at any time to show the sword, with the hilt a little bent. There were several more that had been equally great in the field, not one of whom but was persuaded that he had a considerable hand in bringing the war to a happy termination.

But all these were nothing to the tales of ghosts and apparitions that succeeded. The neighborhood is rich in legendary treasures of the kind. Local tales and superstitions thrive best in these sheltered long-settled retreats; but are trampled underfoot by the shifting throng that forms the population of most of our country places. Besides, there is no encouragement for ghosts in most of our villages, for they have scarcely had time to finish their first nap, and turn themselves in their graves before their surviving friends have travelled away from the neighborhood; so that when they turn out at night to walk their rounds, they have no acquaintance left to call upon. This is perhaps the reason why we so seldom hear of ghosts, except in our long-established Dutch communities.

The immediate cause, however, of the prevalence of supernatural stories in these parts was doubtless owing to the vicinity of Sleepy Hollow. There was a contagion in the very air that blew from the haunted region; it breathed forth an atmosphere of dreams and fancies infecting all the land. Several of the Sleepy Hollow people were present at Van Tassel's and, as usual, were doling out their wild and wonderful legends. Many dismal tales were told about funeral trains, and mourning cries and wailings heard and seen about the great tree where the unfortunate Major André was taken, and which stood in the neighborhood. Some mention was made also of the woman in white, that haunted the dark glen at Raven Rock, and was often heard to shriek on winter nights before a storm, having perished there in the snow. The chief part of the stories, however, turned upon the favorite spectre of Sleepy Hollow, the headless horseman, who had been heard several times of late, patrolling the country; and, it was said, tethered his horse nightly among the graves in the churchyard.

The sequestered situation of this church seems always to have made it a favorite haunt of troubled spirits. It stands on a knoll, surrounded by locust-trees and lofty elms, from among which its decent whitewashed walls shine modestly forth, like Christian purity beaming through the shades of retirement. A gentle slope descends from it to a silver sheet of water, bordered by high trees, between which, peeps may be caught at the blue hills of the Hudson. To look upon its grass-grown yard, where the sunbeams seem to sleep so quietly, one would think that there at least the dead might rest in peace. On one side of the church extends a wide woody dell, along which raves a large brook among broken rocks and trucks of fallen trees. Over a deep black part of the stream, not far from the church, was formerly thrown a wooden bridge; the road that led to it, and the bridge itself, were thickly shaded by overhanging trees, which cast a gloom about it, even in the daytime, but occasioned a fearful darkness at night. This was one of the favorite haunts of the headless horseman; and the place where he was most frequently encountered. The tale was told of old Brouwer, a most heretical disbeliever in ghosts, how he met the horseman returning from his foray into Sleepy Hollow, and was obliged to get up behind him; how they galloped over bush and brake, over hill and swamp, until they reached the bridge; when the horseman suddenly turned into a skeleton, threw old Brouwer into the brook, and sprang away over the tree-tops with a clap of thunder.

This story was immediately matched by a thrice marvellous adventure of Brom Bones, who made light of the galloping Hessian as an arrant jockey. He affirmed that, on returning one night from the neighboring village of Sing Sing, he had been overtaken by this midnight trooper; that he had offered to race with him for a bowl of punch, and should have won it too, for Daredevil beat the goblin horse all hollow, but, just as they came to the church bridge, the Hessian bolted, and vanished in a flash of fire.

All these tales, told in that drowsy undertone with which men talk in the dark, the countenances of the listeners only now and then receiving a casual gleam from the glare of a pipe, sank deep in the mind of Ichabod. He repaid them in kind with large extracts from his invaluable author, Cotton Mather, and added many marvellous events that had taken place in his native State of Connecticut, and fearful sights which he had seen in his nightly walks about the Sleepy Hollow.

The revel now gradually broke up. The old farmers gathered together their families in their wagons, and were heard for some time rattling along the hollow roads, and over the distant hills. Some of the damsels mounted on pillions behind their favorite swains, and their light-hearted laughter, mingling with the clatter of hoofs, echoed along the silent woodlands, sounding fainter and fainter until they gradually died away–and the late scene of noise and frolic was all silent and deserted. Ichabod only lingered behind, according to the custom of country lovers, to have a tête-à-tête with the heiress, fully convinced that he was now on the high road to success. What passed at this interview I will not pretend to say, for in fact I do not know. Something, however, I fear me, must have gone wrong, for he certainly sallied forth, after no very great interval, with an air quite desolate and chop-fallen.—Oh, these women! these women! Could that girl have been playing off any of her coquettish tricks?—Was her encouragement of the poor pedagogue all a mere sham to secure her conquest of his rival?—Heaven only knows, not I!—Let it suffice to say, Ichabod stole forth with the air of one who had been sacking a hen-roost, rather than a fair lady's heart. Without looking to the right or left to notice the scene of rural wealth on which he had so often gloated, he went straight to the stable, and with several hearty cuffs and kicks, roused his steed most uncourteously from the comfortable quarters in which he was soundly sleeping, dreaming of mountains of corn and oats, and whole valleys of timothy and clover.

It was the very witching time of night that Ichabod, heavy-hearted and crestfallen, pursued his travel homewards, along the sides of the lofty hills which rise above Tarry Town, and which he had traversed so cheerily in the afternoon. The hour was as dismal as himself. Far below him, the Tappan Zee spread its dusky and indistinct waste of waters, with here and there the tall mast of a sloop riding quietly at anchor under the land. In the dead hush of midnight he could even hear the barking of the watch-dog from the opposite shore of the Hudson; but it was so vague and faint as only to give an idea of his distance from this faithful companion of man. Now and then, too, the long-drawn crowing of a cock, accidentally awakened, would sound far, far off, from some farm-house away among the hills–but it was like a dreaming sound in his ear. No signs of life occurred near him, but occasionally the melancholy chirp of a cricket, or perhaps the gutteral twang of a bull-frog, from a neighboring marsh, as if sleeping uncomfortably, and turning suddenly in his bed.

All the stories of ghosts and goblins that he had heard in the afternoon, now came crowding upon his recollection. The night grew darker and darker; the stars seemed to sink deeper in the sky, and driving clouds occasionally hid them from his sight. He had never felt so lonely and dismal. He was, moreover, approaching the very place where many of the scenes of the ghost-stories had been laid. In the centre of the road stood an enormous tulip-tree, which towered like a giant above all the other trees of the neighborhood, and formed a kind of landmark. Its limbs were gnarled, and fantastic, large enough to form trunks for ordinary trees, twisting down almost to the earth, and rising again into the air. It was connected with the tragical story of the unfortunate André, who had been taken prisoner hard by; and was universally known by the name of Major André's tree. The common people regarded it with a mixture of respect and superstition, partly out of sympathy for the fate of its ill-starred namesake, and partly from the tales of strange sights and doleful lamentations told concerning it.

As Ichabod approached this fearful tree, he began to whistle: he thought his whistle was answered,—it was but a blast sweeping sharply through the dry branches. As he approached a little nearer, he thought he saw something white, hanging in the midst of the tree,—he paused and ceased whistling; but on looking more narrowly, perceived that it was a place where the tree had been scathed by lightning, and the white wood laid bare. Suddenly he heard a groan,—his teeth chattered and his knees smote against the saddle: it was but the rubbing of one huge bough upon another, as they were swayed about by the breeze. He passed the tree in safety; but new perils lay before him.

About two hundred yards from the tree a small brook crossed the road, and ran into a marshy and thickly wooded glen, known by the name of Wiley's swamp. A few rough logs, laid side by side, served for a bridge over this stream. On that side of the road where the brook entered the wood, a group of oaks and chestnuts, matted thick with wild grape-vines, threw a cavernous gloom over it. To pass this bridge was the severest trial. It was at this identical spot that the unfortunate André was captured, and under the covert of those chestnuts and vines were the sturdy yeomen concealed who surprised him. This has ever since been considered a haunted stream, and fearful are the feelings of the school boy who has to pass it alone after dark.

As he approached the stream, his heart began to thump; he summoned up, however, all his resolution, gave his horse half a score of kicks in the ribs, and attempted to dash briskly across the bridge; but instead of starting forward, the per-verse old animal made a lateral movement, and ran broad-side against the fence. Ichabod, whose fears increased with the delay, jerked the reins on the other side, and kicked lusti-ly with the contrary foot: it was all in vain; his steed started, it is true, but it was only to plunge to the opposite side of the road into a thicket of brambles and alder bushes. The school-master now bestowed both whip and heel upon the starveling ribs of old Gunpowder, who dashed forward, snuffling and snorting, but came to a stand just by the bridge, with a suddenness that had nearly sent his rider sprawling over his head. Just at this moment a plashy tramp by the side of the bridge caught the sensitive ear of Ichabod. In the dark shadow of the grove, on the margin of the brook, he beheld something huge, misshapen, black, and towering. It stirred not, but seemed gathered up in the gloom, like some gigan-tic monster ready to spring upon the traveller.

The hair of the affrighted pedagogue rose upon his head

with terror. What was to be done? To turn and fly was now too late; and besides, what chance was there of escaping ghost or goblin, if such it was, which could ride upon the wings of the wind? Summoning up, therefore, a show of courage, he demanded in stammering accents—"Who are you?" He received no reply. He repeated his demand in a still more agitated voice. Still there was no answer. Once more he cudgelled the sides of the inflexible Gunpowder, and, shutting his eyes, broke forth with involuntary fervor into a psalm-tune. Just then the shadowy object of alarm put itself in motion, and, with a scramble and a bound, stood at once in the middle of the road. Though the night was dark and dismal, yet the form of the unknown might now in some degree be ascertained. He appeared to be a horseman of large dimensions, and mounted on a black horse of powerful frame. He made no offer of molestation or sociability, but kept aloof on one side of the road, jogging along on the blind side of old Gunpowder, who had now got over his fright and waywardness.

Ichabod, who had no relish for this strange midnight companion, and bethought himself of the adventure of Brom Bones with the Galloping Hessian, now quickened his steed, in hopes of leaving him behind. The stranger, however, quickened his horse to an equal pace. Ichabod pulled up, and fell into a walk, thinking to lag behind,—the other did the same. His heart began to sink within him; he endeavored to resume his psalm-tune, but his parched tongue clove to the roof of his mouth, and he could not utter a stave. There was something in the moody and dogged silence of this pertinacious companion, that was mysterious and appalling. It was soon fearfully accounted for. On mounting a rising ground, which brought the figure of his fellow-traveller in relief against the sky, gigantic in height, and muffled in a cloak, Ichabod was horror-struck, on perceiving that he was head-less!—but his horror was still more increased, on observing that the head, which should have rested on his shoulders, was carried before him on the pommel of the saddle: his ter-ror rose to desperation; he rained a shower of kicks and blows upon Gunpowder, hoping, by a sudden movement, to give his companion the slip,–but the spectre started full jump with him. Away then they dashed, through thick and thin; stones flying, and sparks flashing at every bound. Ichabod's flimsy garments fluttered in the air, as he stretched his long lank body away over his horse's head, in the eagerness of his flight.

They had now reached the road which turns off to Sleepy Hollow; but Gunpowder, who seemed possessed with a demon, instead of keeping up it, made an opposite turn, and plunged headlong downhill to the left. This road leads through a sandy hollow, shaded by trees for about a quarter of a mile, where it crosses the bridge famous in goblin story, and just beyond swells the green knoll on which stands the whitewashed church.

As yet the panic of the steed had given his unskilful rider an apparent advantage in the chase; but just as he had got half-way through the hollow, the girths of the saddle gave way, and he felt it slipping from under him. He seized it by the pommel, and endeavored to hold it firm, but in vain;

and had just time to save himself by clasping old Gunpowder round the neck, when the saddle fell to the earth, and he heard it trampled underfoot by his pursuer. For a moment, the terror of Hans Van Ripper's wrath passed across the mind–for it was his Sunday saddle; but this was no time for petty fears; the goblin was hard on his haunches; and (unskilful rider that he was!) he had much ado to maintain his seat; sometimes slipping on one side; sometimes on another, and sometimes jolted on the high ridge of his horse's backbone, with a violence that he verily feared would cleave him asunder.

An opening in the trees now cheered him with the hopes that the church-bridge was at hand. The wavering reflection of a silver star in the bosom of the brook told him that he was not mistaken. He saw the walls of the church dimly glaring under the trees beyond. He recollected the place where Brom Bones' ghostly competitor had disappeared. "If I can but reach that bridge," thought Ichabod, "I am safe." Just then he heard the black steed panting and blowing close behind him; he even fancied that he felt his hot breath. Another convulsive kick in the ribs, and old Gunpowder sprang upon the bridge; he thundered over the resounding planks; he gained the opposite side; and now Ichabod cast a look behind to see if his pursuer should vanish, according to rule, in a flash of fire and brimstone. Just then he saw the goblin rising in his stirrups, and in the very act of hurling his head at him. Ichabod endeavored to dodge the horrible missile, but too late. It encountered his cranium with a tremendous crash,–he was tumbled headlong into the dust, and Gunpowder, the black steed, and the goblin rider, passed by like a whirlwind.

The next morning the old horse was found without his saddle, and with the bridle under his feet, soberly cropping the grass at his master's gate. Ichabod did not make his appearance at breakfast;—dinner-hour came, but no Ichabod. The boys assembled at the school-house, and strolled idly about the banks of the brook; but no schoolmaster. Hans Van Ripper now began to feel some uneasiness about the fate of poor Ichabod, and his saddle. An inquiry was set on foot, and after diligent investigation they came upon his traces. In one part of the road leading to the church was found the saddle trampled in the dirt; the tracks of horses' hoofs deeply dented in the road, and evidently at furious speed, were traced to the bridge, beyond which, on the bank of a broad part of the brook, where the water ran deep and black, was found the hat of the unfortunate Ichabod, and close beside it a shattered pumpkin.

The brook was searched, but the body of the schoolmaster was not to be discovered. Hans Van Ripper, as executor of his estate, examined the bundle which contained all his worldly effects. They consisted of two shirts and a half; two stocks for the neck; a pair or two of worsted stockings, an old pair of corduroy small-clothes; a rusty razor; a book of psalm-tunes, full of dogs' ears; and a broken pitch-pipe. As to the books and furniture of the school-house, they belonged to the community, excepting Cotton Mather's *History of Witchcraft,* a *New England Almanac,* and a book of dreams and fortune-telling; in which last was a sheet of foolscap much scribbled and blotted in several fruitless attempts to make a copy of verses in honor of the heiress of Van Tassel. These magic books and the poetic scrawl were forthwith consigned to the flames by Hans Van Ripper; who from that time forward determined to send his children no more to school; observing, that he never knew any good come of this same reading and writing. Whatever money the schoolmaster possessed, and he had received his quarter's pay but a day or two before, he must have had about his person at the time of his disappearance.

The mysterious event caused much speculation at the church on the following Sunday. Knots of gazers and gossips were collected in the churchyard, at the bridge, and at the spot where the hat and pumpkin had been found. The stories of Brouwer, of Bones, and a whole budget of others, were called to mind; and when they had diligently considered them all, and compared them with the symptoms of the present case, they shook their heads, and came to the conclusion that Ichabod had been carried off by the Galloping Hessian. As he was a bachelor, and in nobody's debt, nobody troubled his head any more about him. The school was removed to a different quarter of the Hollow, and another pedagogue reigned in his stead.

It is true, an old farmer, who had been down to New York on a visit several years after, and from whom this account of the ghastly adventure was received, brought home the intelligence that Ichabod Crane was still alive; that he had left the neighborhood, partly through fear of the goblin and Hans

Van Ripper, and partly in mortification at having been suddenly dismissed by the heiress; that he had changed his quarters to a distant part of the country; had kept school and studied law at the same time; had been admitted to the bar, turned politician, electioneered, written for the newspapers, and finally had been made a justice of the Ten Pound Court. Brom Bones too, who shortly after his rival's disappearance conducted the blooming Katrina in triumph to the altar, was observed to look exceedingly knowing whenever the story of Ichabod was related, and always burst into a hearty laugh at the mention of the pumpkin; which led some to suspect that he knew more about the matter than he chose to tell.

The old country wives, however, who are the best judges of these matters, maintain to this day that Ichabod was spirited away by supernatural means; and it is a favorite story often told about the neighborhood round the winter evening fire. The bridge became more than ever an object of superstitious awe, and that may be the reason why the road has been altered of late years, so as to approach the church by the border of the millpond. The school-house, being deserted, soon fell to decay, and was reported to be haunted by the ghost of the unfortunate pedagogue; and the plough-boy, loitering homeward of a still summer evening, has often fancied his voice at a distance, chanting a melancholy psalm-tune, among the tranquil solitudes of Sleepy Hollow.

Washington Irving's

POSTSCRIPT,

Found in the Handwriting of Mr. Knickerbocker.

The preceding Tale is given, almost in the precise words in which I heard it related at a Corporation meeting of the ancient city of Manhattoes, at which were present many of its sagest and most illustrious burghers. The narrator was a pleasant, shabby, gentlemanly old fellow, in pepper-and-salt clothes, with a sadly humorous face; and one whom I strongly suspected of being poor,—he made such efforts to be entertaining. When his story was concluded, there was much laughter and approbation, particularly from two or three deputy aldermen, who had been asleep the greater part of the time. There was, however, one tall, dry-looking old gentleman, with beetling eyebrows, who maintained a grave and rather severe face throughout; now and then folding his arms, inclining his head, and looking down upon the floor, as if turning a doubt over his mind. He was one of your wary men, who never laugh, but on good grounds—when they have reason and the law on their side. When the mirth of the rest of the company had subsided and silence was restored, he leaned one arm on the elbow of his chair, and sticking the other akimbo, demanded, with a slight but exceedingly sage motion of the head, and contraction of the brow, what was the moral of the story, and what it went to prove?

The story-teller, who was just putting a glass of wine to his lips, as a refreshment after his toils, paused for a moment, looked at his inquirer with an air of infinite deference, and, lowering the glass slowly to the table, observed, that the story was intended most logically to prove:

"There is no situation in life but has its advantages and pleasures—provided we will but take a joke as we find it;

"That, therefore, he that runs races with goblin troopers is likely to have rough riding of it.

"*Ergo*, for a country schoolmaster to be refused the hand of a Dutch heiress, is a certain step to high preferment in the state."

The cautious old gentleman knit his brows tenfold closer after this explanation, being sorely puzzled by ratiocination of the syllogism; while, methought, the one in pepper-and-salt eyed him with something of a triumphant leer. At length he observed, that all this was very well, but still he thought the story a little on the extravagant—there were one or two points on which he had his doubts.

"Faith, sir," replied the story-teller, "as to that matter, I don't believe one half of it myself."

D.K.

From The Sketch Book

Rip Van Winkle

A Posthumous Writing of Diedrich Knickerbocker

By Woden, God of Saxons,
From whence comes Wensday, that is Wodensday,
Truth is a thing that ever I will keep
Unto thylke day in which I creep into
My sepulchre—

Cartwright

The following Tale was found among the papers of the late Diedrich Knickerbocker, an old gentleman of New York, who was very curious in the Dutch history of the province, and the manners of the descendants from its primitive settlers. His historical researches, however, did not lie so much among books as among men; for the former are lamentably scanty on his favorite topics; whereas he found the old burghers, and still more their wives, rich in that legendary lore so invaluable to true history. Whenever, therefore, he happened upon a genuine Dutch family, snugly shut up in its low-roofed farmhouse, under a spreading sycamore, he looked upon it as a little clasped volume of black-letter, and studied it with the zeal of a book-worm.

The result of all these researches was a history of the province during the reign of the Dutch governors, which he published some years since. There have been various opinions as to the literary character of his work, and, to tell the truth, it is not a whit better than it should be. Its chief merit is its scrupulous accuracy, which indeed was a little questioned on its first appearance, but has since been completely established; and it is now admitted into all historical collections as a book of unquestionable authority.

The old gentleman died shortly after the publication of his work; and now that he is dead and gone, it cannot do much harm to his memory to say that his time might have been much better employed in weightier labors. He, however, was apt to ride his hobby his own way; and though it did now and then kick up the dust a little in the eyes of his neighbors, and grieve the spirit of some friends, for whom he felt the truest deference and affection, yet his errors and follies are remembered "more in sorrow than in anger," and it begins to be suspected that he never intended to offend. But however his memory may be appreciated by critics, it is still held dear by many folk whose good opinion is well worth having; particularly by certain biscuit-makers, who have gone so far as to imprint his likeness on their New-Year cakes; and have thus given him a chance for immortality, almost equal to being stamped on a Waterloo Medal, or a Queen Anne's Farthing.

Rip Van Winkle

Whoever has made a voyage up the Hudson must remember the Kaatskill mountains. They are a dismembered branch of the great Appalachian family, and are seen away to the west of the river, swelling up to a noble height, and lording it over the surrounding country. Every change of season, every change of weather, indeed, every hour of the day, produces some change in the magical hues and shapes of these mountains, and they are regarded by all the good wives, far and near, as perfect barometers. When the weather is fair and settled, they are clothed in blue and purple, and print their bold outlines on the clear evening sky; but sometimes, when the rest of the landscape is cloudless, they will gather a hood of gray vapors about their summits, which, in the last rays of the setting sun, will glow and light up like a crown of glory.

At the foot of these fairy mountains, the voyager may have descried the light smoke curling up from a village, whose shingle-roofs gleam among the trees, just where the blue tints of the upland melt away into the fresh green of the nearer landscape. It is a little village, of great antiquity, having been founded by some of the Dutch colonists in the early times of the province, just about the beginning of the government of the good Peter Stuyvesant (may he rest in peace!), and there were some of the houses of the original settlers standing within a few years, built of small yellow bricks brought from Holland, having latticed windows and gable fronts, surmounted with weathercocks.

In that same village, and in one of these very houses (which, to tell the precise truth, was sadly time-worn and weather-beaten), there lived, many years since, while the country was yet a province of Great Britain, a simple, good-natured fellow, of the name of Rip Van Winkle. He was a descendant of the Van Winkles who figured so gallantly in the chivalrous days of Peter Stuyvesant, and accompanied him to the siege of Fort Christina. He inherited, however, but little of the martial character of his ancestors. I have observed that he was a simple, good-natured man; he was, moreover, a kind neighbor, and an obedient, hen-pecked husband. Indeed, to the latter circumstance might be owing that meekness of spirit which gained him such universal popularity; for those men are most apt to be obsequious and conciliating abroad, who are under the discipline of shrews at home. Their tempers, doubtless, are rendered pliant and malleable in the fiery furnace of domestic tribulation; and a curtain-lecture is worth all the sermons in the world for teaching the virtues of patience and long-suffering. A termagant wife may, therefore, in some respects, be considered a tolerable blessing; and if so, Rip Van Winkle was thrice blessed.

Certain it is, that he was a great favorite among all the good wives of the village, who, as usual with the amiable sex, took his part in all family squabbles; and never failed, whenever they talked those matters over in their evening gossipings, to lay all the blame on Dame Van Winkle. The children of the village, too, would shout with joy whenever he approached. He assisted at their sports, made their playthings, taught them to fly kites and shoot marbles, and told them long stories of ghosts, witches, and Indians. Whenever he went dodging about the village, he was surrounded by a troop of them, hanging on his skirts, clambering on his back, and playing a thousand tricks on him with impunity; and not a dog would bark at him throughout the neighborhood.

The great error in Rip's composition was an insuperable aversion to all kinds of profitable labor. It could not be from the want of assiduity or perseverance; for he would sit on a wet rock, with a rod as long and heavy as a Tartar's lance, and fish all day without a murmur, even though he should not be encouraged by a single nibble. He would carry a fowling-piece on his shoulder for hours together, trudging through woods and swamps, and up hill and down dale, to shoot a few squirrels or wild pigeons. He would never refuse to assist a neighbor even in the roughest toil, and was a foremost man at all country frolics for husking Indian corn, or building stone fences; the women of the village, too, used to employ him to run their errands, and to do such little odd jobs as their less obliging husbands would not do for them. In a word, Rip was ready to attend to anybody's business but his own; but as to doing family duty, and keeping his farm in order, he found it impossible.

In fact, he declared it was of no use to work on his farm; it was the most pestilent little piece of ground in the whole country; everything about it went wrong, and would go wrong, in spite of him. His fences were continually falling to pieces; his cow would either go astray, or get among the cabbages; weeds were sure to grow quicker in his fields than anywhere else; the rain always made a point of setting in just as he had some out-door work to do; so that though his patrimonial estate had dwindled away under his management, acre by acre, until there was little more left than a mere patch of Indian corn and potatoes, yet it was the worst conditioned farm in the neighborhood.

His children, too, were as ragged and wild as if they belonged to nobody. His son Rip, an urchin begotten in his own likeness, promised to inherit the habits, with the old clothes, of his father. He was generally seen trooping like a colt at his mother's heels, equipped in a pair of his father's cast-off galligaskins, which he had much ado to hold up with one hand, as a fine lady does her train in bad weather.

Rip Van Winkle, however, was one of those happy mortals, of foolish, well-oiled dispositions, who take the world easy, eat white bread or brown, whichever can be got with least thought or trouble, and would rather starve on a penny than work for a pound. If left to himself, he would have whistled life away in perfect contentment; but his wife kept continually dinning in his ears about his idleness, his carelessness, and the ruin he was bringing on his family. Morning, noon, and night, her tongue was incessantly going, and everything he said or did was sure to produce a torrent of household eloquence. Rip had but one way of replying to all lectures of the kind, and that, by frequent use, had grown into a habit. He shrugged his shoulders, shook his head, cast up his eyes, but said nothing. This, however, always provoked a fresh volley from his wife; so that he was fain to draw off his forces, and take to the outside of the house—the only side which, in truth, belongs to a hen-pecked husband.

Rip's sole domestic adherent was his dog Wolf, who was as much hen-pecked as his master; for Dame Van Winkle regarded them as companions in idleness, and even looked upon Wolf with an evil eye, as the cause of his master's going so often astray. True it is, in all points of spirit befitting an honorable dog, he was as courageous an animal as ever scoured the woods; but what courage can withstand the ever-enduring and all-besetting terrors of a woman's tongue? The moment Wolf entered the house his crest fell, his tail drooped to the ground, or curled between his legs, he sneaked about with a gallows air, casting many a sidelong glance at Dame Van Winkle, and at the least flourish of a broomstick or ladle he would fly to the door with yelping precipitation.

Times grew worse and worse with Rip Van Winkle as years of matrimony rolled on; a tart temper never mellows with age, and a sharp tongue is the only edged tool that grows keener with constant use. For a long while he used to console himself, when driven from home, by frequenting a kind of perpetual club of the sages, philosophers, and other idle personages of the village, which held its sessions on a bench before a small inn, designated by a rubicund portrait of His Majesty George the Third. Here they used to sit in the shade through a long, lazy summer's day, talking listlessly over village gossip, or telling endless sleepy stories about nothing. But it would have been worth any statesman's money to have heard the profound discussions that some-times took place, when by chance an old newspaper fell into their hands from some passing traveller. How solemnly they would listen to the contents, as drawled out by Derrick Van Bummel, the schoolmaster, a dapper learned little man, who was not to be daunted by the most gigantic word in the dictionary; and how sagely they would deliberate upon public events some months after they had taken place.

The opinions of this junto were completely controlled by Nicholas Vedder, patriarch of the village, and landlord of the inn, at the door of which he took his seat from morning till night, just moving sufficiently to avoid the sun and keep in the shade of a large tree; so that the neighbors could tell the hour by his movements as accurately as by a sun-dial. It is true he was rarely heard to speak, but smoked his pipe incessantly. His adherents, however (for every great man has his adherents), perfectly understood him, and knew how to gather his opinions. When anything that was read or related displeased him, he was observed to smoke his pipe vehemently, and to send forth short, frequent, and angry puffs; but when pleased, he would inhale the smoke slowly and tranquilly, and emit it in light and placid clouds; and sometimes, taking the pipe from his mouth, and letting the fragrant vapor curl about his nose, would gravely nod his head in token of perfect approbation.

From even this stronghold the unlucky Rip was at length routed by his termagant wife, who would suddenly break in upon the tranquillity of the assemblage and call the members all to naught; nor was that august personage, Nicholas Vedder himself, sacred from the daring tongue of this terrible virago, who charged him outright with encouraging her husband in habits of idleness.

Poor Rip was at last reduced almost to despair; and his only alternative, to escape from the labor of the farm and clamor of his wife, was to take gun in hand and stroll away into the woods. Here he would sometimes seat himself at the foot of a tree, and share the contents of his wallet with Wolf, with whom he sympathized as a fellow-sufferer in persecution. "Poor Wolf," he would say, "thy mistress leads thee a dog's life of it, but never mind, my lad, whilst I live thou shalt never want a friend to stand by thee!" Wolf would wag his tail, look wistfully in his master's face, and if dogs can feel pity, I verily believe he reciprocated the sentiment with all his heart.

In a long ramble of the kind on a fine autumnal day, Rip had unconsciously scrambled to one of the highest parts of the Kaatskill mountains. He was after his favorite sport of squirrel-shooting, and the still solitudes had echoed and re-echoed with the reports of his gun. Panting and fatigued, he threw himself, late in the afternoon, on a green knoll, covered with mountain herbage, that crowned the brow of a precipice. From an opening between the trees he could over-look all the lower country for many a mile of rich woodland. He saw at a distance the lordly Hudson, far, far below him, moving on its silent but majestic course, with the reflection of a purple cloud, or the sail of a lagging bark, here and there sleeping on its glassy bosom, and at last losing itself in the blue highlands.

On the other side he looked down into a deep mountain glen, wild, lonely, and shagged, the bottom filled with frag-ments from the impending cliffs, and scarcely lighted by the reflected rays of the setting sun. For some time Rip lay mus-ing on this scene; evening was gradually advancing; the mountains began to throw their long blue shadows over the valleys; he saw that it would be dark long before he could reach the village, and he heaved a heavy sigh when he thought of encountering the terrors of Dame Van Winkle.

As he was about to descend, he heard a voice from a distance, hallooing, "Rip Van Winkle, Rip Van Winkle!" He looked around, but could see nothing but a crow winging its solitary flight across the mountain. He thought his fancy must have deceived him, and turned again to descend, when he heard the same cry ring through the still evening air: "Rip Van Winkle! Rip Van Winkle!"—at the same time Wolf bristled up his back, and giving a low growl, skulked to his master's side, looking fearfully down into the glen. Rip now felt a vague apprehension stealing over him; he looked anxiously in the same direction, and perceived a strange figure slowly toiling up the rocks, and bending under the weight of something he carried on his back. He was surprised to see any human being in this lonely and unfrequented place; but supposing it to be some one of the neighborhood in need of his assistance, he hastened down to yield it.

On nearer approach he was still more surprised at the singularity of the stranger's appearance. He was a short, square-built old fellow, with thick bushy hair, and a grizzled beard. His dress was of the antique Dutch fashion,–a cloth jerkin strapped around the waist–several pair of breeches, the outer one of ample volume, decorated with rows of buttons down the sides, and bunches at the knees. He bore on his shoulders a stout keg, that seemed full of liquor, and made signs for Rip to approach and assist him with the load. Though rather shy and distrustful of this new acquaintance, Rip complied with his usual alacrity; and mutually relieving one another, they clambered up a narrow gully, apparently the dry bed of a mountain torrent. As they ascended, Rip every now and then heard long, rolling peals, like distant thunder, that seemed to issue out of a deep ravine, or rather cleft, between lofty rocks, toward which their rugged path conducted. He paused for an instant, but supposing it to be the muttering of one of those transient thunder-showers which often take place in mountain heights, he proceeded. Passing through the ravine, they came to a hollow, like a small amphitheatre, surrounded by perpendicular precipices, over the brinks of which impending trees shot their branches, so that you only caught glimpses of the azure sky and the bright evening cloud. During the whole time Rip and his companion had labored on in silence; for though the former marvelled greatly what could be the object of carrying a keg of liquor up this wild mountain, yet there was something strange and incomprehensible about the unknown, that inspired awe and checked familiarity.

On entering the amphitheatre, new objects of wonder presented themselves. On a level spot in the centre was a company of odd-looking personages playing at ninepins. They were dressed in a quaint, outlandish fashion; some wore short doublets, others jerkins, with long knives in their belts, and most of them had enormous breeches, of similar style with that of the guide's. Their visages, too, were peculiar: one had a large beard, broad face, and small piggish eyes; the face of another seemed to consist entirely of nose, and was surmounted by a white sugar-loaf hat, set off with a little red cock's tail. They all had beards, of various shapes and colors. There was one who seemed to be the commander. He was a stout old gentleman, with a weather-beaten countenance; he wore a laced doublet, broad belt and hanger, high crowned hat and feather, red stockings, and high-heeled shoes, with roses in them. The whole group reminded Rip of the figures in an old Flemish painting, in the parlor of Dominie Van Shaick, the village parson, and which had been brought over from Holland at the time of the settlement.

What seemed particularly odd to Rip was, that, though these folks were evidently amusing themselves, yet they maintained the gravest faces, the most mysterious silence, and were, withal, the most melancholy party of pleasure he had ever witnessed. Nothing interrupted the stillness of the scene but the noise of the balls, which, whenever they rolled, echoed along the mountains like rumbling peals of thunder.

As Rip and his companion approached them, they suddenly desisted from their play, and stared at him with such fixed, statue-like gaze, and such strange, uncouth, lack-lustre countenances, that his heart turned within him, and his knees smote together. His companion now emptied the contents of the keg into large flagons, and made signs to him to wait upon the company. He obeyed with fear and trembling; they quaffed the liquor in profound silence, and then returned to their game.

By degrees Rip's awe and apprehension subsided. He even ventured, when no eye was fixed upon him, to taste the beverage, which he found had much of the flavor of excellent

Hollands. He was naturally a thirsty soul, and was soon tempted to repeat the draught. One taste provoked another; and he reiterated his visits to the flagon so often that at length his senses were overpowered, his eyes swam in his head, his head gradually declined, and he fell into a deep sleep.

On waking, he found himself on the green knoll whence he had first seen the old man of the glen. He rubbed his eyes—it was a bright sunny morning. The birds were hopping and twittering among the bushes, and the eagle was wheeling aloft, and breasting the pure mountain breeze. "Surely," thought Rip, "I have not slept here all night." He recalled the occurrences before he fell asleep. The strange man with a keg of liquor—the mountain ravine—the wild retreat among the rocks—the woe-begone party at ninepins—the flagon—"Oh! that flagon! that wicked flagon!" thought Rip, "what excuse shall I make to Dame Van Winkle?"

He looked round for his gun, but in place of the clean, well-oiled fowling piece, he found an old firelock lying by him, the barrel encrusted with rust, the lock falling off, and the stock worm-eaten. He now suspected that the grave roisters of the mountains had put a trick upon him, and, having dosed him with liquor, had robbed him of his gun. Wolf, too, had disappeared, but he might have strayed away after a squirrel or partridge. He whistled after him, and shouted his name, but all in vain; the echoes repeated his whistle and shout, but no dog was to be seen.

He determined to revisit the scene of the last evening's

gambol, and if he met with any of the party, to demand his dog and gun. As he rose to walk, he found himself stiff in the joints, and wanting in his usual activity. "These mountain beds do not agree with me," thought Rip, "and if this frolic should lay me up with a fit of the rheumatism, I shall have a blessed time with Dame Van Winkle." With some difficulty he got down into the glen: he found the gully up which he and his companion had ascended the preceding evening; but to his astonishment a mountain stream was now foaming down it, leaping from rock to rock, and filling the glen with babbling murmurs. He, however, made shift to scramble up its sides, working his toilsome way through thickets of birch, sassafras, and witch-hazel, and sometimes tripped up or entangled by the wild grape-vines that twisted their coils or tendrils from tree to tree, and spread a kind of network in his path.

At length he reached to where the ravine had opened through the cliffs to the amphitheatre; but no traces of such opening remained. The rocks presented a high, impenetrable wall, over which the torrent came tumbling in a sheet of feather foam, and fell into a broad deep basin, black from the shadows of the surrounding forest. Here, then, poor Rip was brought to a stand. He again called and whistled after his dog; he was only answered by the cawing of a flock of idle crows, sporting high in the air about a dry tree that overhung a sunny precipice; and who, secure in their elevation, seemed to look down and scoff at the poor man's perplexities. What was to be done? The morning was passing away, and Rip felt famished for want of his breakfast. He grieved to give up his dog and gun; he dreaded to meet his wife; but it would not do to starve among the mountains. He shook his head, shouldered the rusty firelock, and, with a heart full of trouble and anxiety, turned his footsteps homeward.

As he approached the village he met a number of people, but none whom he knew, which somewhat surprised him, for he had thought himself acquainted with every one in the country round. Their dress, too, was of a different fashion from that to which he was accustomed. They all stared at him with equal marks of surprise, and whenever they cast their eyes upon him, invariably stroked their chins. The constant recurrence of this gesture induced Rip, involuntarily, to do the same, when to his astonishment, he found his beard had grown a foot long!

He had now entered the skirts of the village. A troop of strange children ran at his heels, hooting after him, and pointing at his gray beard. The dogs, too, not one of which he recognized for an old acquaintance, barked at him as he passed. The very village was altered; it was larger and more populous. There were rows of houses which he had never seen before, and those which had been his familiar haunts had disappeared. Strange names were over the doors—strange faces at the windows—everything was strange. His mind now misgave him; he began to doubt whether both he and the world around him were not bewitched. Surely this was his native village, which he had left but the day before. There stood the Kaatskill mountains—there ran the silver Hudson at a distance—there was every hill and dale precisely as it had always been. Rip was sorely perplexed. "That flagon last night," thought he, "has addled my poor head sadly!"

It was with some difficulty that he found the way to his own house, which he approached with silent awe, expecting every moment to hear the shrill voice of Dame Van Winkle. He found the house gone to decay—the roof fallen in, the windows shattered, and the doors off the hinges. A half-starved dog that looked like Wolf was skulking about it. Rip called him by name, but the cur snarled, showed his teeth, and passed on. This was an unkind cut indeed. "My very dog," sighed poor Rip, "has forgotten me!"

He entered the house, which to tell the truth, Dame Van Winkle had always kept in neat order. It was empty, forlorn, and apparently abandoned. This desolateness overcame all his connubial fears—he called loudly for his wife and children—the lonely chambers rang for a moment with his voice, and then all again was silence.

He now hurried forth, and hastened to his old resort, the village inn, but it too was gone. A large rickety wooden building stood in its place, with great gaping windows, some of them broken and mended with old hats and petticoats, and over the door was painted, "The Union Hotel, by Jonathan Doolittle." Instead of the great tree that used to shelter the quiet little Dutch inn of yore, there now was reared a tall naked pole, with something on top that looked like a red night-cap, and from it was fluttering a flag, on which was a singular assemblage of stars and stripes;—all this was strange and incomprehensible. He recognized on

He now suspected that the grave roisters of the mountains had put a trick upon him....

the sign, however, the ruby face of King George, under which he had smoked so many a peaceful pipe; but even this was singularly metamorphosed. The red coat was changed for one of blue and buff, a sword was held in the hand instead of a sceptre, the head was decorated with a cocked hat, and underneath was painted in large characters, GENERAL WASHINGTON.

There was, as usual, a crowd of folk about the door, but none that Rip recollected. The very character of the people seemed changed. There was a busy, bustling, disputatious tone about it, instead of the accustomed phlegm and drowsy tranquillity. He looked in vain for the sage Nicholas Vedder, with his broad face, double chin, and fair long pipe, uttering clouds of tobacco-smoke instead of idle speeches; or Van Bummel, the schoolmaster, doling forth the contents of an ancient newspaper. In place of these, a lean, bilious-looking fellow, with his pockets full of handbills, was haranguing vehemently about rights of citizens—elections—members of congress—liberty—Bunker's Hill—heroes of seventy-six— and other words, which were a perfect Babylonish jargon to the bewildered Van Winkle.

The appearance of Rip, with his long, grizzled beard, his rusty fowling-piece, his uncouth dress, and an army of women and children at his heels, soon attracted the attention of the tavern-politicians. They crowded around him, eying him from head to foot with great curiosity. The orator bustled up to him, and, drawing him partly aside, inquired "On which side he voted?" Rip stared in vacant stupidity. Another short but busy little fellow pulled him by the arm, and, rising on tiptoe, inquired in his ear, "Whether he was Federal or Democrat?" Rip was equally at a loss to comprehend the question; when a knowing, self-important old gentleman, in a sharp cocked hat, made his way through the crowd, putting them to the right and left with his elbows as he passed, and planting himself before Van Winkle, with one arm akimbo, the other resting on his cane, his keen eyes and sharp hat penetrating, as it were, into his very soul, demanded in an austere tone, "What brought him to the election with a gun on his shoulder, and a mob at his heels; and whether he meant to breed a riot in the village?"—"Alas! gentlemen," cried Rip, somewhat dismayed, "I am a poor quiet man, a native of the place, and a loyal subject of the King, God bless him!"

Here a general shout burst from the by-standers—"A tory! a tory! a spy! a refugee! hustle him! away with him!" It was with great difficulty that the self-important man in the cocked hat restored order; and, having assumed a tenfold austerity of brow, demanded again of the unknown culprit, what he came there for, and whom he was seeking? The poor man humbly assured him that he meant no harm, but merely came there in search of some of his neighbors, who used to keep about the tavern.

"Well—who are they?—name them."

Rip bethought himself a moment, and inquired, "Where's Nicholas Vedder?"

There was a silence for a little while, when an old man replied, in a thin piping voice, "Nicholas Vedder! why, he is dead and gone these eighteen years! There was a wooden tombstone in that churchyard that used to tell all about him, but that's rotten and gone too."

"Where's Brom Dutcher?"

"Oh, he went off to the army in the beginning of the war; some say he was killed at the storming of Stony Point—others say he was drowned in a squall at the foot of Antony's Nose. I don't know—he never came back again."

"Where's Van Bummel, the schoolmaster?"

"He went off to the wars too, was a great militia general, and is now in congress."

Rip's heart died away at hearing of these sad changes in his home and friends, and finding himself thus alone in the world. Every answer puzzled him too, by treating of such enormous lapses of time, and of matters which he could not understand: war—congress—Stony Point—he had no courage to ask after any more friends, but cried out in despair, "Does nobody here know Rip Van Winkle?"

"Oh, Rip Van Winkle!" exclaimed two or three, "oh, to be sure! that's Rip Van Winkle yonder, leaning against the tree."

Rip looked, and he beheld a precise counterpart of himself, as he went up the mountain, apparently as lazy, and certainly as ragged. The poor fellow was now completely confounded. He doubted his own identity, and whether he was himself or another man. In the midst of his bewilderment, the man in the cocked hat demanded who he was, and what was his name.

"God knows," exclaimed he, at his wit's end; "I'm not myself—I'm somebody else—that's me yonder—no—that's somebody else got into my shoes—I was myself last night, but I fell asleep on the mountain, and they've changed my gun, and everything's changed, and I'm changed, and I can't tell what's my name, or who I am!"

The by-standers began now to look at each other, nod, wink significantly, and tap their fingers against their fore-heads. There was a whisper, also, about securing the gun, and keeping the old fellow from doing mischief, at the very suggestion of which the self-important man in the cocked hat retired with some precipitation. At this critical moment a fresh, comely woman pressed through the throng to get a peep at the gray-bearded man. She had a chubby child in her arms, which, frightened at his looks, began to cry. "Hush, Rip," cried she, "hush, you little fool; the old man won't hurt you." The name of the child, the air of the mother, the tone of her voice, all awakened a train of recollections in his mind. "What is your name, my good woman?" asked he.

"Judith Gardenier."

"And your father's name?"

"Ah, poor man, Rip Van Winkle was his name, but it's twenty years since he went away from home with his gun, and never has been heard of since,—his dog came home without him; but whether he shot himself, or was carried away by the Indians, nobody can tell. I was then but a little girl."

Rip had but one question more to ask; but he put it with a faltering voice:

"Where's your mother?"

"Oh, she too had died but a short time since; she broke a bloodvessel in a fit of passion at a New England pedler."

Rip Van Winkle

There was a drop of comfort, at least, in this intelligence. The honest man could contain himself no longer. He caught his daughter and her child in his arms. "I am your father!" cried he—"Young Rip Van Winkle once—old Rip Van Winkle now!—Does nobody know poor Rip Van Winkle?"

All stood amazed, until an old woman, tottering out from among the crowd, put her hand to her brow, and peering under it in his face for a moment, exclaimed, "Sure enough! it is Rip Van Winkle—it is himself! Welcome home again, old neighbor. Why, where have you been these twenty long years?"

Rip's story was soon told, for the whole twenty years had been to him but as one night. The neighbors stared when they heard it; some were seen to wink at each other, and put their tongues in their cheeks: and the self-important man in the cocked hat, who, when the alarm was over, had returned to the field, screwed down the corners of his mouth, and shook his head—upon which there was a general shaking of the head throughout the assemblage.

It was determined, however, to take the opinion of old Peter Vanderdonk, who was seen slowly advancing up the road. He was a descendant of the historian of that name, who wrote one of the earliest accounts of the province. Peter was the most ancient inhabitant of the village, and well versed in all the wonderful events and traditions of the neighborhood. He recollected Rip at once, and corroborated his story in the most satisfactory manner. He assured the company that it was a fact, handed down from his ancestor the historian, that the Kaatskill mountains had always been haunted by strange beings. That it was affirmed that the great Hendrick Hudson, the first discoverer of the river and country, kept a kind of vigil there every twenty years, with his crew of the Half-moon; being permitted in this way to revisit the scenes of his enterprise, and keep a guardian eye upon the river and the great city called by his name. That his father had once seen them in their old Dutch dresses playing at ninepins in a hollow of the mountain; and that he himself had heard, one summer afternoon, the sound of their balls, like distant peals of thunder.

To make a long story short, the company broke up and returned to the more important concerns of the election. Rip's daughter took him home to live with her; she had a snug, well-furnished house, and a stout, cheery farmer for a husband, whom Rip recollected for one of the urchins that used to climb upon his back. As to Rip's son and heir, who was the ditto of himself, seen leaning against the tree, he was employed to work on the farm; but evinced an hereditary disposition to attend to anything else but his business.

Rip now resumed his old walks and habits; he soon found many of his former cronies, though all rather the worse for the wear and tear of time; and preferred making friends among the rising generation, with whom he soon grew into great favor.

Having nothing to do at home, and being arrived at that happy age when a man can be idle with impunity, he took his place once more on the bench at the inn-door, and was reverenced as one of the patriarchs of the village, and a chronicle of the old times "before the war." It was some time before he could get into the regular track of gossip, or could be made to comprehend the strange events that had taken place during his torpor. How that there had been a revolutionary war,—that the country had thrown off the yoke of old England,—and that, instead of being a subject of his Majesty George the Third, he was now a free citizen of the United States. Rip, in fact, was no politician; the changes of states and empires made but little impression on him; but there was one species of despotism under which he long groaned, and that was—petticoat government. Happily that was at an end; he had got his neck out of the yoke of matrimony, and could go in and out whenever he pleased, without dreading the tyranny of Dame Van Winkle. Whenever her name was mentioned, however, he shook his head, shrugged his shoulders, and cast up his eyes; which might pass either for an expression of resignation to his fate, or joy at his deliverance.

He used to tell his story to every stranger that arrived at Mr. Doolittle's hotel. He was observed, at first, to vary on some points every time he told it, which was, doubtless, owing to his having so recently awaked. It at last settled down precisely to the tale I have related, and not a man, woman, or child in the neighborhood but knew it by heart. Some always pretended to doubt the reality of it, and insisted that Rip had been out of his head, and that this was one point on which he always remained flighty. The old Dutch inhabitants, however, almost universally gave it full credit. Even to this day they never hear a thunderstorm of a summer afternoon about the Kaatskill, but they say Hendrick Hudson and his crew are at their game of ninepins; and it is a common wish of all hen-pecked husbands in the neighborhood, when life hangs heavy on their hands, that they might have a quieting draught out of Rip Van Winkle's flagon.

Note:

The foregoing Tale, one would suspect, had been suggested to Mr. Knickerbocker by a little German superstition about the Emperor Frederick der Rothbart, and the Kypphäuser mountain: the subjoined note, however, which he had appended to the tale, shows that it is an absolute fact, narrated with his usual fidelity.

"The story of Rip Van Winkle may seem incredible to many, but nevertheless I give it my full belief, for I know the vicinity of our old Dutch settlements to have been very subject to marvellous events and appearances. Indeed, I have heard many stranger stories than this, in the villages along the Hudson; all of which were too well authenticated to admit of a doubt. I have even talked with Rip Van Winkle myself, who, when last I saw him, was a very venerable old man, and so perfectly rational and consistent on every other point, that I think no conscientious person could refuse to take this into the bargain; nay, I have seen a certificate on the subject taken before a country justice and signed with a cross, in the justice's own handwriting. The story, therefore, is beyond the possibility of doubt.

"D.K."

The Spectre Bridegroom

A Traveller's Tale

"Shall I not take mine ease in mine inn!"
                    FALSTAFF.

During a journey that I once made through the Netherlands, I had arrived one evening at the Pomme d' Or, the principal inn of a small Flemish village. It was after the hour of the table d'hôte, so that I was obliged to make a solitary supper from the relics of its ampler board. The weather was chilly; I was seated alone in one end of a great gloomy dining-room, and, my repast being over, I had the prospect before me of a long dull evening, without any visible means of enlivening it. I summoned mine host, and requested something to read; he brought me the whole literary stock of his household, a Dutch family Bible, an almanac in the same language, and a number of old Paris newspapers. As I sat dozing over one of the latter, reading old and stale criticisms, my ear was now and then struck with bursts of laughter which seemed to proceed from the kitchen. Every one that has travelled on the continent must know how favorite a resort the kitchen of a country inn is to the middle and inferior order of travellers; particularly in that equivocal kind of weather, when a fire becomes agreeable toward evening. I threw aside the newspaper, and explored my way to the kitchen, to take a peep at the group that appeared to be so merry. It was composed partly of travellers who had arrived some hours before in a diligence, and partly of the usual attendants and hangers-on of inns. They were seated round a great burnished stove, that might have been mistaken for an altar, at which they were worshipping. It was covered with various kitchen vessels of resplendent brightness; among which steamed and hissed a huge copper tea-kettle. A large lamp threw a strong mass of light upon the group, bringing out many odd features in strong relief. Its yellow rays partially illumined the spacious kitchen, dying duskily away into remote corners, except where they settled, in mellow radiance on the broad side of a flitch of bacon, or were reflected back from well-scoured utensils, that gleamed from the midst of obscurity. A strapping Flemish lass, with long golden pendants in her ears, and a necklace with a golden heart suspended to it, was the presiding priestess of the temple.

Many of the company were furnished with pipes, and most of them with some kind of evening potation. I found their mirth was occasioned by anecdotes, which a little swarthy Frenchman, with a dry weazen face and large whiskers, was giving of his love adventures; at the end of each of which there was one of those bursts of honest unceremonious laughter, in which a man indulges in that temple of true liberty, an inn.

As I had no better mode of getting through a tedious blustering evening, I took my seat near the stove, and listened to a variety of traveller's tales, some very extravagant, and most very dull. All of them, however, have faded from my treacherous memory except one, which I will endeavor to relate. I fear, however, it derived its chief zest from the manner in which it was told, and the peculiar air and appearance of the narrator. He was a corpulent old Swiss, who had the look of a veteran traveller. He was dressed in a tarnished green travelling-jacket, with a broad belt round his waist, and a pair of overalls, with buttons from the hips to the ankles. He was of a full, rubicund countenance, with a double chin, aquiline nose and a pleasant, twinkling eye. His hair was light, and curled from under an old green velvet travelling-cap stuck on one side of his head. He was interrupted more than once by the arrival of guests, or the remarks of his auditors; and paused now and then to replenish his pipe; at which times he had generally a roguish leer, and a sly joke for the buxom kitchen-maid.

I wish my readers could imagine the old fellow lolling in a huge armchair, one arm akimbo, the other holding a curiously twisted tobacco-pipe, formed of genuine *écume de mer*, decorated with silver chain and silken tassel,–his head cocked on one side, and a whimsical cut of the eye occasionally, as he related the following story.

He that supper for is dight,
He lyes full cold, I trow, this night!
Yestreen to chamber I him led,
This night Gray-Steel has made his bed.
Sir Eger, Sir Grahame, and Sir Gray-Steel.

On the summit of one of the heights of the Odenwald, a wild and romantic tract of Upper Germany, that lies not far from the confluence of the Main and the Rhine, there stood, many, many years since, the Castle of the Baron Von Landshort. It is now quite fallen to decay, and almost buried among beechtrees and dark firs; above which, however, its old watch-tower may still be seen struggling, like the former possessor I have mentioned, to carry a high head, and look down upon the neighboring country.

The baron was a dry branch of the great family of Katzenellenbogen, and inherited the relics of the property, and all the pride of his ancestors. Though the warlike disposition of his predecessors had much impaired the family possessions, yet the baron still endeavored to keep up some show of former state. The times were peaceable, and the German nobles, in general, had abandoned their inconvenient old castles, perched like eagles' nests among the mountains, and had built more convenient residences in the valleys: still the baron remained proudly drawn up in his little fortress, cherishing, with hereditary inveteracy, all the old family feuds; so that he was on ill terms with some of his nearest neighbors, on account of disputes that had happened between their great-great-grandfathers.

The baron had but one child, a daughter; but nature, when she grants but one child, always compensates by making it a prodigy; and so it was with the daughter of the baron. All the nurses, gossips, and country-cousins assured her father that she had not her equal for beauty in all Germany; and who should know better than they? She had, moreover, been brought up with great care under the superintendence of two maiden aunts, who had spent some years of their early life at one of the little German courts, and were skilled in all the branches of knowledge necessary to the education of a fine lady. Under their instructions she became a miracle of accomplishments. By the time she was eighteen, she could embroider to admiration, and had worked whole histories of the saints in tapestry, with such strength of expression in their countenance, that they looked like so many souls in purgatory. She could read without great difficulty, and had spelled her way through several church legends, and almost all the chivalric wonders of the Heldenbuch. She had even made considerable proficiency in writing; could sign her own name without missing a letter, and so legibly that her aunts could read it without spectacles. She excelled in making little elegant good-for-nothing lady-like knickknacks of all kinds; was versed in the most abstruse dancing of the day; played a number of airs on the harp and guitar; and knew all the tender ballads of the Minnelieders by heart.

Her aunts, too, having been great flirts and coquettes in

their younger days, were admirably calculated to be vigilant guardians and strict censors of the conduct of their niece; for there is no duenna so rigidly prudent, and inexorably decorous, as a superannuated coquette. She was rarely suffered out of their sight; never went beyond the domains of the castle, unless well attended, or rather well watched; had continual lectures read to her about strict decorum and implicit obedience; and as to the men—pah!—she was taught to hold them at such a distance, and in such absolute distrust, that, unless properly authorized, she would not have cast a glance upon the handsomest cavalier in the world—no, not if he were even dying at her feet.

The good effects of this system were wonderfully apparent. The young lady was a pattern of docility and correctness. While others were wasting their sweetness in the glare of the world, and liable to be plucked and thrown aside by every hand, she was coyly blooming into fresh and lovely womanhood under the protection of those immaculate spinsters like a rose-bud blushing forth among guardian thorns. Her aunts looked upon her with pride and exultation, and vaunted that though all the other young ladies in the world might go astray, yet, thank Heaven, nothing of the kind could happen to the heiress of Katzenellenbogen.

But, however scantily the Baron Von Landshort might be provided with children, his household was by no means a small one; for Providence had enriched him with an abundance of poor relations. They, one and all, possessed the affectionate disposition common to humble relatives; were wonderfully attached to the baron, and took every possible occasion to come in swarms and enliven the castle. All family festivals were commemorated by these good people at the baron's expense; and when they were filled with good cheer, they would declare that there was nothing on earth so delightful as these family meetings, these jubilees of the heart.

The baron, though a small man, had a large soul, and it swelled with satisfaction at the consciousness of being the greatest man in the little world about him. He loved to tell long stories about the dark old warriors whose portraits looked grimly down from the walls around, and he found no listeners equal to those who fed at his expense. He was much given to the marvellous, and a firm believer in all those supernatural tales with which every mountain and valley in Germany abounds. The faith of his guests exceeded even his own; they listened to every tale of wonder with open eyes and mouth, and never failed to be astonished, even though repeated for the hundredth time. Thus lived the Baron Von Landshort, the oracle of his table, the absolute monarch of his little territory, and happy, above all things, in the persuasion that he was the wisest man of the age.

At the time of which my story treats, there was a great family-gathering at the castle, on an affair of the utmost importance: it was to receive the destined bridegroom of the baron's daughter. A negotiation had been carried on between the father and an old nobleman of Bavaria, to unite the dignity of their houses by the marriage of their children. The preliminaries had been conducted with proper punctilio. The young people were betrothed without seeing each other; and the time was appointed for the marriage ceremony. The young Count Von Altenburg had been recalled from the army for the purpose, and was actually on his way to the baron's to receive his bride. Missives had even been received from him, from Würtzburg, where he was accidentally detained, mentioning the day and hour when he might be expected to arrive.

The castle was in a tumult of preparation to give him a suitable welcome. The fair bride had been decked out with uncommon care. The two aunts had superintended her toilet, and quarrelled the whole morning about every article of her dress. The young lady had taken advantage of their contest to follow the bent of her own taste; and fortunately it was a good one. She looked as lovely as youthful bridegroom could desire; and the flutter of expectation heightened the lustre of her charms.

The suffusions that mantled her face and neck, the gentle heaving of the bosom, the eye now and then lost in reverie, all betrayed the soft tumult that was going on in her little heart. The aunts were continually hovering around her; for maiden aunts are apt to take great interest in affairs of this nature. They were giving her a world of staid counsel how to deport herself, what to say, and in what manner to receive the expected lover.

The baron was no less busied in preparations. He had, in truth, nothing exactly to do; but he was naturally a fuming, bustling little man, and could not remain passive when all the world was in a hurry. He worried from top to bottom of the castle with an air of infinite anxiety; he continually called the servants from their work to exhort them to be diligent;

and buzzed about every hall and chamber, as idly restless and importunate as a blue-bottle fly on a warm summer's day.

In the meantime the fatted calf had been killed; the forests had rung with the clamor of the huntsmen; the kitchen was crowded with good cheer; the cellars had yielded up whole oceans of Rhein-wein and Ferne-wein; and even the great Heidelberg tun had been laid under contribution. Everything was ready to receive the distinguished guest with Saus and Braus in the true spirit of German hospitality;—but the guest delayed to make his appearance. Hour rolled after hour. The sun, that had poured his downward rays upon the rich forest of the Odenwald, now just gleamed along the summits of the mountains. The baron mounted the highest tower, and strained his eyes in the hope of catching a distant sight of the count and his attendants. Once he thought he beheld them; the sound of horns came floating from the valley, prolonged by the mountain echoes. A number of horsemen were seen far below, slowly advancing along the road; but when they had nearly reached the foot of the mountain, they suddenly struck off in a different direction. The last ray of sunshine departed,—the bats begin to flit by in the twilight,—the road grew dimmer and dimmer to the view, and nothing appeared stirring in it but now and then a peasant lagging homeward from his labor.

While the old castle of Landshort was in this state of perplexity, a very interesting scene was transacting in a different part of the Odenwald.

The young Count Von Altenburg was tranquilly pursuing

his route in that sober jogtrot way, in which a man travels toward matrimony when his friends have taken all the trouble and uncertainty of courtship off his hands, and a bride is waiting for him, as certainly as a dinner at the end of his journey. He had encountered at Würtzburg a youthful companion in arms, with whom he had seen some service on the frontiers,—Herman Von Starkenfaust, one of the stoutest hands and worthiest hearts of German chivalry, who was now returning from the army. His father's castle was not far distant from the old fortress of Landshort, although an hereditary feud rendered the families hostile, and strangers to each other.

In the warm-hearted moment of recognition, the young friends related all their past adventures and fortunes, and the count gave the whole history of his intended nuptials with a young lady whom he had never seen, but of whose charms he had received the most enrapturing descriptions.

As the route of the friends lay in the same direction, they agreed to perform the rest of their journey together; and, that they might do it the more leisurely, set off from Würtzburg at an early hour, the count having given directions for his retinue to follow and overtake him.

They beguiled their wayfaring with recollections of their military scenes and adventures; but the count was apt to be a little tedious, now and then, about the reputed charms of his bride, and the felicity that awaited him.

In this way they had entered among the mountains of the Odenwald, and were traversing one of its most lonely and thickly-wooded passes. It is well known that the forests of

Germany have always been as much infested by robbers, as its castles by spectres; and, at this time, the former were particularly numerous, from the hordes of disbanded soldiers wandering about the country. It will not appear extraordinary, therefore, that the cavaliers were attacked by a gang of these stragglers, in the midst of the forest. They defended themselves with bravery, but were nearly over-powered, when the count's retinue arrived to their assis-tance. At sight of them the robbers fled, but not until the count had received a mortal wound. He was slowly and carefully conveyed back to the city of Würtzburg, and a friar summoned from a neighboring convent, who was famous for his skill in administering to both soul and body; but half of his skill was superfluous; the moments of the unfortunate count were numbered.

With his dying breath he entreated his friend to repair instantly to the castle of Landshort, and explain the fatal cause of his not keeping his appointment with his bride. Though not the most ardent of lovers, he was one of the most punctilious of men, and appeared earnestly solicitous that his mission should be speedily and courteously executed. "Unless this is done," said he, "I shall not sleep quietly in my grave!" He repeated these last words with peculiar solemni-ty. A request, at a moment so impressive, admitted no hesita-tion. Starkenfaust endeavored to soothe him to calmness; promised faithfully to execute his wish, and gave him his hand in solemn pledge. The dying man pressed it in acknowledgment, but soon lapsed into delirium—raved about his bride—his engagements—his plighted word;

ordered his horse, that he might ride to the castle of Landshort; and expired in the fancied act of vaulting into the saddle.

Starkenfaust bestowed a sigh and a soldier's tear on the untimely fate of his comrade; and then pondered on the awkward mission he had undertaken. His heart was heavy, and his head perplexed; for he was to present himself an unbidden guest among hostile people, and to damp their festivity with tidings fatal to their hopes. Still there were certain whisperings of curiosity in his bosom to see this far-famed beauty of Katzenellenbogen, so cautiously shut up from the world; for he was a passionate admirer of the sex, and there was a dash of eccentricity and enterprise in his character that made him fond of all singular adventure.

Previous to his departure he made all due arrangements with the holy fraternity of the convent for the funeral solemnities of his friend, who was to be buried in the cathedral of Würtzburg, near some of his illustrious relatives; and the mourning retinue of the count took charge of his remains.

It is now high time that we should return to the ancient family of Katzenellenbogen, who were impatient for their guest, and still more for their dinner; and to the worthy little baron, whom we left airing himself on the watch-tower.

Night closed in, but still no guest arrived. The baron descended from the tower in despair. The banquet, which had been delayed from hour to hour, could no longer be postponed. The meats were already overdone; the cook in an agony; and the whole household had the look of a garrison that had been reduced by famine. The baron was obliged reluctantly to give orders for the feast without the presence of the guest. All were seated at table, and just on the point of commencing, when the sound of a horn from without the gate gave notice of the approach of a stranger. Another long blast filled the old courts of the castle with its echoes, and was answered by the warder from the walls. The baron hastened to receive his future son-in-law.

The drawbridge had been let down, and the stranger was before the gate. He was a tall, gallant cavalier, mounted on a black steed. His countenance was pale, but he had a beaming, romantic eye, and an air of stately melancholy. The baron was a little mortified that he should have come in this simple, solitary style. His dignity for a moment was ruffled, and he felt disposed to consider it a want of proper respect for the important occasion, and the important family with which he was to be connected. He pacified himself, however, with the conclusion, that it must have been youthful impatience which had induced him thus to spur on sooner than his attendants.

"I am sorry," said the stranger, "to break in upon you thus unseasonably—"

Here the baron interrupted him with a world of compliments and greetings; for, to tell the truth, he prided himself upon his courtesy and eloquence. The stranger attempted, once or twice, to stem the torrent of words, but in vain, so he bowed his head and suffered it to flow on. By the time the baron had come to a pause, they had reached the inner court of the castle; and the stranger was again about to speak, when he was once more interrupted by the appearance of the female part of the family, leading forth the shrinking and blushing bride. He gazed on her for a moment as one entranced; it seemed as if his whole soul beamed forth in the gaze, and rested upon that lovely form. One of the maiden aunts whispered something in her ear; she made an effort to speak; her moist blue eye was timidly raised; gave a shy glance of inquiry on the stranger and was cast again to the ground. The words died away; but there was a sweet smile playing about her lips, and a soft dimpling of the cheek that showed her glance had not been unsatisfactory. It was impossible for a girl of the fond age of eighteen, highly predisposed for love and matrimony, not to be pleased with so gallant a cavalier.

The late hour at which the guest had arrived left no time for parley. The baron was peremptory, and deferred all particular conversation until the morning, and led the way to the untasted banquet.

It was served up in the great hall of the castle. Around the walls hung the hard-favored portraits of the heroes of the house of Katzenellenbogen, and the trophies which they had gained in the field and in the chase. Hacked corselets, splintered jousting spears, and tattered banners, were mingled with the spoils of sylvan warfare; the jaws of the wolf, and the tusks of the boar, grinned horribly among cross-bows and battle-axes, and a huge pair of antlers branched immediately over the head of the youthful bridegroom.

The cavalier took but little notice of the company or the entertainment. He scarcely tasted the banquet, but seemed absorbed in admiration of his bride. He conversed in a low tone that could not be overheard—for the language of love is never loud; but where is the female ear so dull that it cannot catch the softest whisper of the lover? There was a mingled tenderness and gravity in his manner, that appeared to have a powerful effect upon the young lady. Her color came and went as she listened with deep attention. Now and then she made some blushing reply, and when his eye was turned away, she would steal a sidelong glance at his romantic countenance, and heave a gentle sigh of tender happiness. It was evident that the young couple were completely enamored. The aunts, who were deeply versed in the mysteries of the heart, declared that they had fallen in love with each other at first sight.

The feast went on merrily, or at least noisily, for the guests were all blessed with those keen appetites that attend upon light purses and mountain-air. The baron told his best and longest stories, and never had he told them so well, or with such great effect. If there was anything marvellous, his auditors were lost in astonishment; and if anything facetious, they were sure to laugh exactly in the right place. The baron, it is true, like most great men, was too dignified to utter any joke but a dull one; it was always enforced, however, by a bumper of excellent Hockheimer; and even a dull joke, at one's own table, served up with jolly old wine, is irresistible. Many good things were said by poorer and keener wits, that would not bear repeating, except on similar occasions; many sly speeches whispered in ladies' ears, that almost convulsed them with suppressed laughter; and a song or two roared out by a poor, but merry and broad-faced cousin of the baron, that absolutely made the maiden aunts hold up their fans.

Amidst all this revelry, the stranger guest maintained a most singular and unseasonable gravity. His countenance assumed a deeper caste of dejection as the evening advanced; and, strange as it may appear, even the baron's jokes seemed only to render him the more melancholy. At times he was lost in thought, and at times there was a perturbed and restless wandering of the eye that bespoke a mind but ill at ease. His conversations with the bride became more and more earnest and mysterious. Lowering clouds began to steal over the fair serenity of her brow, and tremors to run through her tender frame.

All this could not escape the notice of the company. Their gayety was chilled by the unaccountable gloom of the bridegroom; their spirits were infected; whispers and glances were interchanged, accompanied by shrugs and dubious shakes of the head. The song and the laugh grew less and less frequent; there were dreary pauses in the conversation, which were at length succeeded by wild tales and supernatural legends. One dismal story produced another still more dismal, and the baron nearly frightened some of the ladies into hysterics with the history of the goblin horseman that carried away the fair Leonora: a dreadful story, which has since been put into excellent verse, and is read and believed by all the world.

The bridegroom listened to this tale with profound attention. He kept his eyes steadily fixed on the baron and, as the story drew to a close, began gradually to rise from his seat, growing taller and taller, until, in the baron's entranced eye, he seemed almost to tower into a giant. The moment the tale was finished, he heaved a deep sigh, and took a solemn farewell of the company. They were all amazement. The baron was perfectly thunderstruck.

"What! going to leave the castle at midnight? why, everything was prepared for his reception; a chamber was ready for him if he wished to retire."

The stranger shook his head mournfully and mysteriously; "I must lay my head in a different chamber to-night!"

There was something in this reply, and the tone in which it was uttered, that made the baron's heart misgive him; but he rallied his forces, and repeated his hospitable entreaties.

The stranger shook his head silently, but positively, at every offer; and, waving his farewell to the company, stalked slowly out of the hall. The maiden aunts were absolutely petrified; the bride hung her head, and a tear stole to her eye.

The baron followed the stranger to the great court of the castle, where the black charger stood pawing the earth, and snorting with impatience. When they had reached the portal, whose deep archway was dimly lighted by a cresset, the stranger paused, and addressed the baron in a hollow tone of voice, which the vaulted roof rendered still more sepulchral.

"Now that we are alone," said he, "I will impart to you the reason of my going. I have a solemn, an indispensable engagement—"

"Why," said the baron, "cannot you send some one in your place?"

"It admits of no substitute—I must attend it in person—I must away to Würtzburg cathedral—"

"Ay," said the baron, plucking up spirit, "but not until to-morrow—to-morrow you shall take your bride there."

"No! no!" replied the stranger, with tenfold solemnity, "my engagement is with no bride—the worms! the worms expect me! I am a dead man—I have been slain by robbers—my body lies at Würtzburg—at midnight I am to be buried—the grave is waiting for me—I must keep my appointment!"

He sprang on his black charger, dashed over the draw-bridge, and the clattering of his horse's hoofs was lost in the whistling of the nightblast.

The baron returned to the hall in the utmost consternation, and related what had passed. Two ladies fainted outright, others sickened at the idea of having banqueted with a spectre. It was the opinion of some, that this might be the wild huntsman, famous in German legend. Some talked of mountain sprites, of wood-demons, and of other supernatural beings, with which the good people of Germany have been so grievously harassed since time immemorial. One of the poor relations ventured to suggest that it might be some sportive evasion of the young cavalier, and that the very gloominess of the caprice seemed to accord with so melancholy a personage. This, however, drew on him the indignation of the whole company, and especially of the baron, who looked upon him as little better than an infidel; so that he was fain to abjure his heresy as speedily as possible, and come into the faith of the true believers.

But whatever may have been the doubts entertained, they

were completely put to an end by the arrival, next day, of regular missives, confirming the intelligence of the young count's murder, and his interment in Würtzburg cathedral.

The dismay at the castle may well be imagined. The baron shut himself up in his chamber. The guests, who had come to rejoice with him, could not think of abandoning him in his distress. They wandered about the courts, or collected in groups in the hall, shaking their heads and shrugging their shoulders, at the troubles of so good a man; and sat longer than ever at table, and ate and drank more stoutly than ever, by way of keeping up their spirits. But the situation of the widowed bride was the most pitiable. To have lost a husband before she had even embraced him—and such a husband! If the very spectre could be so gracious and noble, what must have been the living man. She filled the house with lamentations.

On the night of the second day of her widowhood, she had retired to her chamber, accompanied by one of her aunts, who insisted on sleeping with her. The aunt, who was one of the best tellers of ghost-stories in all Germany, had just been recounting one of her longest, and had fallen asleep in the very midst of it. The chamber was remote, and overlooked a small garden. The niece lay pensively gazing at the beams of the rising moon, as they trembled on the leaves of an aspen tree before the lattice. The castle-clock had just tolled midnight when a soft strain of music stole up from the garden. She rose hastily from her bed, and stepped lightly to the window. A tall figure stood among the shadows of the trees. As it raised its head, a beam of moonlight fell upon the countenance. Heaven and earth! She beheld the Spectre Bridegroom! A loud shriek at that moment burst upon her ear, and her aunt, who had been awakened by the music, and had followed her silently to the window, fell into her arms. When she looked again, the spectre had disappeared.

Of the two females, the aunt now required the most soothing, for she was perfectly beside herself with terror. As to the young lady, there was something, even in the spectre of her lover, that seemed endearing. There was still the semblance of manly beauty; and though the shadow of a man is but little calculated to satisfy the affections of a lovesick girl, yet, where the substance is not to be had, even that is consoling. The aunt declared she would never sleep in that chamber again; the niece, for once, was refractory, and declared as strongly that she would sleep in no other in the castle: the consequence was, that she had to sleep in it alone; but she drew a promise from her aunt not to relate the story of the spectre, lest she should be denied the only melancholy pleasure left her on earth—that of inhabiting the chamber over which the guardian shade of her lover kept its nightly vigils.

How long the good old lady would have observed this promise is uncertain, for she dearly loved to talk of the marvellous, and there is a triumph in being the first to tell a frightful story; it is, however, still quoted in the neighborhood, as a memorable instance of female secrecy, that she kept it to herself for a whole week; when she was suddenly absolved from all further restraint, by intelligence brought to the breakfast-table one morning that the young lady was not to be found. Her room was empty—the bed had not been slept in—the window was open, and the bird had flown!

The astonishment and concern with which the intelligence was received can only be imagined by those who have witnessed the agitation which the mishaps of a great man cause among his friends. Even the poor relations paused for a moment from the indefatigable labors of the trencher; when the aunt, who had at first been struck speechless, wrung her hands, and shrieked out, "The goblin! the goblin! she's carried away by the goblin!"

In a few words she related the fearful scene in the garden, and concluded that the spectre must have carried off his bride. Two of the domestics corroborated the opinion, for they had heard the clattering of a horse's hoofs down the mountain about midnight, and had no doubt that it was the spectre on his black charger, bearing her away to the tomb. All present were struck with the direful probability; for events of the kind are extremely common in Germany, as many well-authenticated histories bear witness.

What a lamentable situation was that of the poor baron! What a heart-rending dilemma for a fond father, and a member of the great family of Katzenellenbogen! His only daughter had either been rapt away to the grave, or he was to have some wood-demon for a son-in-law, and perchance, a troop of goblin grandchildren. As usual, he was completely bewildered, and all the castle in an uproar. The men were ordered to take horse, and scour every road and path and glen of the Odenwald. The baron himself had just drawn on his jack-boots, girded on his sword, and was about to mount his steed and sally forth on a doubtful quest, when he was brought to a pause by a new apparition. A lady was seen approaching the castle, mounted on a palfrey, attended by a cavalier on horseback. She galloped up to the gate, sprang from her horse, and falling at the baron's feet, embraced his knees. It was his lost daughter, and her companion—the Spectre Bridegroom! The baron was astounded. He looked at his daughter, then at the spectre, and almost doubted the evidence of his senses. The latter, too, was wonderfully improved in his appearance since his visit to the world of spirits. His dress was splendid, and set off a noble figure of manly symmetry. He was no longer pale and melancholy. His fine countenance was flushed with the glow of youth, and joy rioted in his large dark eye.

The mystery was soon cleared up. The cavalier (for, in truth, as you must have known all the while, he was no goblin) announced himself as Sir Herman Von Starkenfaust. He related his adventure with the young count. He told how he had hastened to the castle to deliver the unwelcome tidings, but that the eloquence of the baron had interrupted him in every attempt to tell his tale. How the sight of the bride had completely captivated him, and that to pass a few hours near her, he had tacitly suffered the mistake to continue. How he had been sorely perplexed in what way to make a decent retreat, until the baron's goblin stories had suggested his eccentric exit. How, fearing the feudal hostility of the family, he had repeated his visits by stealth—had haunted the garden beneath the young lady's window—had wooed—had won—had borne away in triumph—and, in a word, had wedded the fair.

Under any other circumstances the baron would have been inflexible, for he was tenacious of paternal authority, and devoutly obstinate in all family feuds; but he loved his daughter; he had lamented her as lost; he rejoiced to find her still alive; and, though her husband was of a hostile house, yet, thank heaven, he was not a goblin. There was something, it must be acknowledged, that did not exactly accord with his notions of strict veracity, in the joke the knight had passed upon him of his being a dead man; but several old friends present, who had served in the wars, assured him that every strategem was excusable in love, and that the cavalier was entitled to especial privilege, having lately served as a trooper.

Matters, therefore, were happily arranged. The baron pardoned the young couple on the spot. The revels at the castle were resumed. The poor relations overwhelmed this new member of the family with loving-kindness; he was so gallant, so generous—and so rich. The aunts, it is true, were somewhat scandalized that their system of strict seclusion and passive obedience should be so badly exemplified, but attributed it all to their negligence in not having the windows grated. One of them was particularly mortified at having her marvellous story marred, and that the only spectre she had ever seen should turn out a counterfeit; but the niece seemed perfectly happy at having found him substantial flesh and blood—and so the story ends.

From The Sketch Book

The Hunting-Dinner

I was once at a hunting-dinner, given by a worthy fox-hunting old Baronet, who kept bachelor's hall in jovial style in an ancient rook-haunted family-mansion, in one of the middle counties. He had been a devoted admirer of the fair sex in his younger days; but, having travelled much, studied the sex in various countries with distinguished success, and returned home profoundly instructed, as he supposed, in the ways of woman, and a perfect master of the art of pleasing, had the mortification of being jilted by a little boarding-school girl, who was scarcely versed in the accidence of love.

The Baronet was completely overcome by such an incredible defeat; retired from the world in disgust; put himself under the government of his housekeeper; and took to fox-hunting like a perfect Nimrod. Whatever poets may say to the contrary, a man will grow out of love as he grows old; and a pack of fox-hounds may chase out of his heart even the memory of a boarding-school goddess. The Baronet was, when I saw him, as merry and mellow an old bachelor as ever followed a hound; and the love he had once felt for one woman had spread itself over the whole sex, so that there was not a pretty face in the whole country round but came in for a share.

The dinner was prolonged till a late hour; for our host having no ladies in his household to summon us to the drawing-room, the bottle maintained its true bachelor sway, unrivalled by its potent enemy, the tea-kettle. The old hall in which we dined echoed to bursts of robustious fox-hunting merriment, that made the ancient antlers shake on the walls. By degrees, however, the wine and the wassail of mine host began to operate upon bodies already a little jaded by the chase. The choice spirits which flashed up at the beginning of the dinner, sparkled for a time, then gradually went out one after another, or only emitted now and then a faint gleam from the socket. Some of the briskest talkers, who had given tongue so bravely at the first burst, fell fast asleep; and none kept on their way but certain of those long-winded prosers, who, like short-legged hounds, worry on unnoticed at the bottom of conversation, but are sure to be in at the death. Even these at length subsided into silence; and scarcely anything was heard but the nasal communications of two or three veteran masticators, who having been silent while awake, were indemnifying the company in their sleep.

At length the announcement of tea and coffee in the cedar-parlor roused all hands from this temporary torpor. Every one awoke marvellously renovated, and while sipping the refreshing beverage out of the Baronet's old-fashioned hereditary china, began to think of departing for their several homes. But here a sudden difficulty arose. While we had been prolonging our repast, a heavy winter storm had set in, with snow, rain, and sleet, driven by such bitter blasts of wind, that they threatened to penetrate to the very bone.

"It's all in vain," said our hospitable host, "to think of putting one's head out of doors in such weather. So, gentlemen, I hold you my guests for this night at least, and will have your quarters prepared accordingly."

The unruly weather, which became more and more tempestuous, rendered the hospitable suggestion unanswerable. The only question was, whether such an unexpected accession of company to an already crowded house would not put the housekeeper to her trumps to accommodate them.

"Pshaw," cried mine host; "did you ever know a bachelor's hall that was not elastic, and able to accommodate twice as many as it could hold?" So, out of a good-humored pique, the housekeeper was summoned to a consultation before us all. The old lady appeared in her gala suit of faded brocade, which rustled with flurry and agitation; for, in spite of our host's bravado, she was a little perplexed. But in a bachelor's house, and with bachelor guests, these matters are readily managed. There is no lady of the house to stand upon squeamish points about lodging gentlemen in odd holes and corners, and exposing the shabby parts of the establishment. A bachelor's housekeeper is used to shifts and emergencies; so, after much worrying to and fro, and divers consultations about the red-room, and the blue-room, and the chintz-room, and the damask-room, and the little room with the bow-window, the matter was finally arranged.

When all this was done, we were once more summoned to the standing rural amusement of eating. The time that had been consumed in dozing after dinner, and in the refreshment and consultation of the cedar-parlor, was sufficient, in the opinion of the rosy-faced butler, to engender a reasonable appetite for supper. A slight repast, had, therefore, been tricked up from the residue of dinner, consisting of a cold sirloin of beef, hashed venison, a devilled leg of a turkey or so, and a few other of those light articles taken by country gentlemen to ensure sound sleep and heavy snoring.

The nap after dinner had brightened up every one's wit; and a great deal of excellent humor was expended upon the perplexities of mine host and his housekeeper, by certain married gentlemen of the company, who considered themselves privileged in joking with a bachelor's establishment. From this the banter turned as to what quarters each would find, on being thus suddenly billeted in so antiquated a mansion.

"By my soul," said an Irish captain of dragoons, one of the most merry and boisterous of the party, "by my soul, but I should not be surprised if some of those good-looking gentlefolks that hang along the walls should walk about the rooms of this stormy night; or if I should find the ghosts of one of those longwaisted ladies turning into my bed in mistake for her grave in the churchyard."

"Do you believe in ghosts, then?" said a thin, hatchet-faced gentleman, with projecting eyes like a lobster.

I had remarked this last personage during dinner-time for one of those incessant questioners, who have a craving, unhealthy appetite in conversation. He never seemed satisfied with the whole of a story; never laughed when others laughed; but always put the joke to the question. He never could enjoy the kernel of the nut, but pestered himself to get more out of the shell. "Do you believe in ghosts, then?" said the inquisitive gentleman.

"Faith, but I do," replied the jovial Irishman. "I was brought up in the fear and belief of them. We had a Benshee in our own family, honey."

"A Benshee, and what's that?" cried the questioner.

"Why, an old lady ghost that tends upon your real Milesian families, and waits at their window to let them know when some of them are to die."

"A mighty pleasant piece of information!" cried an elderly gentleman with a knowing look, and with a flexible nose, to which he could give a whimsical twist when he wished to be waggish.

"By my soul, but I'd have you to know it's a piece of distinction to be waited on by a Benshee. It's a proof that one had pure blood in one's veins. But i'faith, now we are talking of ghosts, there never was a house or a night better fitted than the present for a ghost adventure. Pray, Sir John, haven't you such a thing as a haunted chamber to put a guest in?"

"Perhaps," said the Baronet, smiling, "I might accomodate you even on that point."

"Oh, I should like it of all things, my jewel. Some dark oaken room, with ugly woe-begone portraits, that stare dismally at one; and about which the housekeeper has a power of delightful stories of love and murder. And then a dim lamp, a table with a rusty sword across it, and a spectre all in white, to draw aside one's curtains at midnight—"

"In truth," said an old gentleman at one end of the table, "you put me in mind of an anecdote—"

"Oh, a ghost-story! a ghost-story!" was vociferated round the board, every one edging his chair a little nearer.

The attention of the whole company was now turned upon the speaker. He was an old gentleman, one side of whose face was no match for the other. The eyelid drooped and hung down like an unhinged window-shutter. Indeed, the whole side of his head was dilapidated, and seemed like the wing of a house shut up and haunted. I'll warrant that side was well stuffed with ghost-stories.

There was a universal demand for the tale.

"Nay," said the old gentleman, "it's a mere anecdote, and a very commonplace one; but such as it is you shall have it. It is a story that I once heard my uncle tell as having happened to himself. He was a man very apt to meet with strange adventures. I have heard him tell of others much more singular."

"What kind of a man was your uncle?" said the questioning gentleman.

"Why, he was rather a dry, shrewd kind of a body; a great traveller, and fond of telling his adventures."

"Pray, how old might he have been when that happened?"

"When what happened?" cried the gentleman with the

flexible nose, impatiently. "Egad, you have not given anything a chance to happen. Come, never mind our uncle's age; let us have his adventures."

The inquisitive gentleman being for the moment silenced, the old gentleman with the haunted head proceeded.

The Adventure of My Uncle

Many years since, some time before the French Revolution, my uncle passed several months at Paris. The English and French were on better terms in those days than at present, and mingled cordially in society. The English went abroad to spend money then, and the French were always ready to help them: they go abroad to save money at present, and that they can do without French assistance. Perhaps the travelling English were fewer and choicer than at present, when the whole nation has broke loose and inundated the continent. At any rate, they circulated more readily and currently in foreign society, and my uncle, during his residence in Paris, made many very intimate acquaintances among the French noblesse.

Some time afterwards, he was making a journey in the winter-time in that part of Normandy called the Pays de Caux, when, as evening was closing in, he perceived the turrets of an ancient chateau rising out of the trees of its walled park; each turret with its high conical roof of gray slate, like a candle with an extinguisher on it.

"To whom does the chateau belong, friend?" cried my uncle to a meagre but fiery postilion, who, with tremendous jack-boots and cocked hat, was floundering on before him.

"To Monseigneur the Marquis de—," said the postilion, touching his hat, partly out of respect to my uncle, and partly out of reverence to the noble name pronounced.

My uncle recollected the Marquis for a particular friend in Paris, who had often expressed a wish to see him at his paternal chateau. My uncle was an old traveller, one who knew well how to turn things to account. He revolved for a few moments in his mind, how agreeable it would be to his friend the Marquis to be surprised in this sociable way by a pop visit; and how much more agreeable to himself to get into snug quarters in a chateau, and have a relish of the Marquis's well-known kitchen, and a smack of his superior Champagne and Burgundy, rather than put up with the miserable lodgment and miserable fare of a provincial inn. In a few minutes, therefore, the meagre postilion was cracking his whip like a very devil, or like a true Frenchman, up the long, straight avenue that led to the chateau.

You have no doubt all seen French chateaus, as everybody travels in France nowadays. This was one of the oldest; standing naked and alone in the midst of a desert of gravel walks and cold stone terraces; with a cold-looking, formal garden, cut into angles and rhomboids; and a cold, leafless park, divided geometrically by straight alleys; and two or three cold-looking noseless statues; and fountains spouting cold water enough to make one's teeth chatter. At least such was the feeling they imparted on the wintry day of my uncle's visit; though, in hot summer weather, I'll warrant there was glare enough to scorch one's eyes out.

The smacking of the postilion's whip, which grew more and more intense the nearer they approached, frightened a flight of pigeons out of a dove-cot, and rooks out of the roofs, and finally a crew of servants out of the chateau, with the Marquis at their head. He was enchanted to see my uncle, for his chateau, like the house of our worthy host, had not many more guests at the time than it could accommodate. So he kissed my uncle on each cheek, after the French fashion, and ushered him into the castle.

The Marquis did the honors of the house with the urbanity of his country. In fact, he was proud of his old family chateau, for part of it was extremely old. There was a tower and chapel which had been built almost before the memory of man; but the rest was more modern, the castle having been nearly demolished during the wars of the league. The Marquis dwelt upon this event with great satisfaction, and seemed really to entertain a grateful feeling towards Henry the Fourth, for having thought his paternal mansion worth battering down. He had many stories to tell of the prowess of his ancestors; and several skull-caps, helmets, and cross-bows, and divers huge boots and buff jerkins, to show, which had been worn by the leaguers. Above all, there was a two-handed sword, which he could hardly wield, but which he displayed, as a proof that there had been giants in his family.

In truth, he was but a small descendant from such great warriors. When you looked at their bluff visages and brawny limbs, as depicted in their portraits, and then at the little

Marquis, with his spindle shanks, and his sallow lantern visage, flanked with a pair of powdered earlocks, or *aîles de pigeon*, that seemed ready to fly away with it, you could hardly believe him to be of the same race. But when you looked at the eyes that sparkled out like a beetle's from each side of his hooked nose, you saw at once that he inherited all the fiery spirit of his forefathers. In fact, a Frenchman's spirit never exhales, however his body may dwindle. It rather rarefies, and grows more inflammable, as the earthly particles diminish; and I have seen valor enough in a little fiery-hearted French dwarf to have furnished out a tolerable giant.

When once the Marquis, as was his wont, put on one of the old helmets stuck up in his hall, though his head no more filled it than a dry pea its peascod, yet his eyes flashed from the bottom of the iron cavern with the brilliancy of carbuncles; and when he poised the ponderous two-handed sword of his ancestors, you would have thought you saw the doughty little David wielding the sword of Goliath, which was unto him like a weaver's beam.

However, gentlemen, I am dwelling too long on this description of the Marquis and his chateau, but you must excuse me; he was an old friend of my uncle; and whenever my uncle told the story, he was always fond of talking a great deal about his host.—Poor little Marquis! He was one of that handful of gallant courtiers who made such a devoted but hopeless stand in the cause of their sovereign, in the chateau of the Tuileries, against the irruption of the mob on the sad tenth of August. He displayed the valor of a *preux* French chevalier to the last; flourishing feebly his little court-sword with a *ça-ça!* in the face of a whole legion of *sans-culottes;* but was pinned to the wall like a butterfly, by the pike of a *poissarde,* and his heroic soul was borne up to heaven on his *aîles de pigeon.*

But all this has nothing to do with my story. To the point, then. When the hour arrived for retiring for the night, my uncle was shown to his room in a venerable old tower. It was the oldest part of the chateau, and had in ancient times been the donjon or stronghold; of course the chamber was none of the best. The Marquis had put him there, however, because he knew him to be a traveller of taste, and fond of antiquities; and also because the better apartments were already occupied. Indeed, he perfectly reconciled my uncle to his quarters by mentioning the great personages who had once inhabited them, all of whom were, in some way or other, connected with the family. If you would take his word for it, John Baliol, or as he called him, Jean de Bailleul, had died of chagrin in this very chamber, on hearing of the success of his rival, Robert de Bruce, at the battle of Bannockburn. And when he added that the Duke de Guise had slept in it, my uncle was fain to felicitate himself on being honored with such distinguished quarters.

The night was shrewd and windy, and the chamber none of the warmest. An old long-faced, long-bodied servant, in quaint livery, who attended upon my uncle, threw down an armful of wood beside the fireplace, gave a queer look about the room, and then wished him *bon repos* with a grimace and a shrug that would have been suspicious from any other than an old French servant.

The chamber had indeed a wild, crazy look, enough to strike any one who had read romances with apprehension and foreboding. The windows were high and narrow, and had once been loop-holes, but had been rudely enlarged, as well as the extreme thickness of the walls would permit; and the ill-fitted casements rattled to every breeze. You would have thought, on a windy night, some of the old leaguers were tramping and clanking about the apartment in their huge boots and rattling spurs. A door which stood ajar, and, like a true French door, would stand ajar in spite of every reason and effort to the contrary, opened upon a long dark corridor, that led the Lord knows whither, and seemed just made for ghosts to air themselves in, when they turned out of their graves at midnight. The wind would spring up into a hoarse murmur through this passage, and creak the door to and fro, as if some dubious ghost were balancing in its mind whether to come in or not. In a word, it was precisely the kind of comfortless apartment that a ghost, if ghost there were in the chateau, would single out for its favorite lounge.

My uncle, however, though a man accustomed to meet with strange adventures, apprehended none at the time. He made several attempts to shut the door, but in vain. Not that he apprehended anything, for he was too old a traveller to be daunted by a wild-looking apartment; but the night, as I have said, was cold and gusty, and the wind howled about the old turret pretty much as it does round this old mansion at this moment, and the breeze from the long dark corridor came in as damp and as chilly as if from a dungeon. My uncle, therefore, since he could not close the door, threw a quantity of wood on the fire, which soon sent up a flame in the great wide-mouthed chimney that illumined the whole chamber; and made the shadow of the tongs on the opposite wall look like a long-legged giant. My uncle now clambered on the top of the half-score of mattresses which form a French bed, and which stood in a deep recess; then tucking himself snugly in, and burying himself up to the chin in the bed-clothes, he lay looking at the fire, and listening to the wind, and thinking how knowingly he had come over his friend the Marquis for a night's lodging – and so he fell asleep.

He had not taken above half of his first nap when he was awakened by the clock of the chateau, in the turret over his chamber, which struck midnight. It was just such an old clock as ghosts are fond of. It had a deep, dismal tone, and struck so slowly and tediously that my uncle thought it would never have done. He counted and counted till he was confident he counted thirteen, and then it stopped.

The fire had burnt low, and the blaze of the last fagot was almost expiring, burning in small blue flames, which now and then lengthened up into little white gleams. My uncle lay with his eyes half closed, and his nightcap drawn almost down to his nose. His fancy was already wandering, and began to mingle up the present scene with the crater of Vesuvius, the French Opera, the Coliseum at Rome, Dolly's chop-house in London, and all the farrago of noted places with which the brain of a traveller is crammed,—in a word, he was just falling asleep.

Suddenly he was roused by the sound of footsteps, slowly pacing along the corridor. My uncle, as I have often heard him say himself, was a man not easily frightened. So he lay quiet, supposing this some other guest, or some servant on his way to bed. The footsteps, however, approached the door; the door gently opened; whether of its own accord, or whether pushed open, my uncle could not distinguish: a figure all in white glided in. It was a female, tall and stately, and of a commanding air. Her dress was of an ancient fashion, ample in volume, and sweeping the floor. She walked up to the fireplace without regarding my uncle, who raised his nightcap with one hand, and stared earnestly at her. She remained for some time standing by the fire, which, flashing up at intervals, cast blue and white gleams of light, that enabled my uncle to remark her appearance minutely.

Her face was ghastly pale, and perhaps rendered still more so by the bluish light of the fire. It possessed beauty, but its beauty was saddened by care and anxiety. There was the look of one accustomed to trouble, but of one whom trouble could not cast down nor subdue; for there was still the predominating air of proud, unconquerable resolution. Such at least was the opinion formed by my uncle, and he considered himself a great physiognomist.

The figure remained, as I said, for some time by the fire, putting out first one hand, then the other; then each foot alternately, as if warming itself; for your ghosts, if ghost it really was, are apt to be cold. My uncle, furthermore, remarked that it wore high-heeled shoes, after an ancient fashion, with paste or diamond buckles, that sparkled as though they were alive. At length the figure turned gently round, casting a glassy look about the apartment, which, as

Heaven and earth! She beheld the Spectre Bridegroom!

it passed over my uncle, made his blood run cold, and chilled the very marrow in his bones. It then stretched its arms towards heaven, clasped its hands, and wringing them in a supplicating manner, glided slowly out of the room.

My uncle lay for some time meditating on this visitation, for (as he remarked when he told me the story) though a man of firmness, he was also a man of reflection, and did not reject a thing because it was out of the regular course of events. However, being, as I have before said, a great traveller, and accustomed to strange adventures, he drew his nightcap resolutely over his eyes, turned his back to the door, hoisted the bedclothes high over his shoulders, and gradually fell asleep.

How long he slept he could not say, when he was awakened by the voice of some one at his bedside. He turned round, and beheld the old French servant, with his ear-locks in tight buckles on each side of a long lantern face, on which habit had deeply wrinkled an everlasting smile. He made a thousand grimaces, and asked a thousand pardons for disturbing Monsieur, but the morning was considerably advanced. While my uncle was dressing, he called vaguely to mind the visitor of the preceding night. He asked the ancient domestic what lady was in the habit of rambling about this part of the chateau at night. The old valet shrugged his shoulders as high as his head, laid one hand on his bosom, threw open the other with every finger extended, made a most whimsical grimace which he meant to be complimentary, and replied, that it was not for him to know anything of *les bonnes fortunes* of Monsieur.

My uncle saw there was nothing satisfactory to be learned in this quarter. After breakfast, he was walking with the Marquis through the modern apartments of the chateau, sliding over the well-waxed floors of silken saloons, amidst furniture rich in gilding and brocade, until they came to a long picture-gallery, containing many portraits, some in oil and some in chalks.

Here was an ample field for the eloquence of his host, who had all the pride of a nobleman of the *ancien régime*. There was not a grand name in Normandy, and hardly one in France, which was not, in some way or other, connected with his house. My uncle stood listening with inward impatience, resting sometimes on one leg, sometimes on the other, as the little Marquis descanted, with his usual fire and vivacity, on the achievements of his ancestors, whose portraits hung along the wall; from the martial deeds of the stern warriors in steel, to the gallantries and intrigues of the blue-eyed gentlemen, with fair smiling faces, powdered ear-locks, laced ruffles, and pink and blue silk coats and breeches;—not forgetting the conquests of the lovely shepherdesses, with hooped petticoats, and waists no thicker than an hourglass, who appeared ruling over their sheep and their swains, with dainty crooks decorated with fluttering ribbons.

In the midst of his friend's discourse, my uncle was startled on beholding a full-length portrait, the very counterpart of his visitor of the preceding night.

"Methinks," said he, pointing to it, "I have seen the original of this portrait."

"*Pardonnez moi,*" replied the Marquis politely, "that can hardly be, as the lady has been dead more than a hundred years. That was the beautiful Duchess de Longueville, who figured during the minority of Louis the Fourteenth."

"And was there anything remarkable in her history?"

Never was question more unlucky. The little Marquis immediately threw himself into the attitude of a man about to tell a long story. In fact, my uncle had pulled upon himself the whole history of the civil war of the Fronde, in which the beautiful Duchess had played so distinguished a part. Turenne, Coligni, Mazarin, were called up from their graves to grace his narration; nor were the affairs of the Barricadoes, nor the chivalry of the Port Cochères forgotten. My uncle began to wish himself a thousand leagues off from the Marquis and his merciless memory, when suddenly the little man's recollections took a more interesting turn. He was relating the imprisonment of the Duke de Longueville with the Princes Condé and Conti in the chateau of Vincennes, and the ineffectual efforts of the Duchess to rouse the sturdy Normans to their rescue. He had come to that part where she was invested by the royal forces in the Castle of Dieppe.

"The spirit of the Duchess," proceeded the Marquis, "rose from her trials. It was astonishing to see so delicate and beautiful a being buffet so resolutely with hardships. She determined on a desperate means of escape. You may have seen the chateau in which she was mewed up,—an old ragged wart of an edifice, standing on the knuckle of a hill, just above the rusty little town of Dieppe. One dark unruly night she issued secretly out of a small postern gate of the castle, which the enemy had neglected to guard. The postern gate is there to this very day; opening upon a narrow bridge over a deep fosse between the castle and the brow of the hill. She was followed by her female attendants, a few domestics, and some gallant cavaliers, who still remained faithful to her fortunes. Her object was to gain a small port about two leagues distant, where she had privately provided a vessel for her escape in case of emergency.

"The little band of fugitives were obliged to perform the distance on foot. When they arrived at the port the wind was high and stormy, the tide contrary, the vessel anchored far off in the road, and no means of getting on board but by a fishing-shallop which lay tossing like a cockle-shell on the edge of the surf. The Duchess determined to risk the attempt. The seamen endeavored to dissuade her but the imminence of her danger on shore, and the magnanimity of her spirit, urged her on. She had to be borne to the shallop in the arms of a mariner. Such was the violence of the wind and waves that he faltered, lost his foothold, and let his precious burden fall into the sea.

"The Duchess was nearly drowned, but partly through her own struggles, partly by the exertions of the seamen, she got to land. As soon as she had a little recovered strength, she insisted on renewing the attempt. The storm, however, had by this time become so violent as to set all efforts at defiance. To delay, was to be discovered and taken prisoner. As the only resource left, she procured horses, mounted with her female attendants, *en croupe*, behind the gallant gentlemen who accompanied her, and scoured the country to seek some temporary asylum.

"While the Duchess," continued the Marquis, laying his forefinger on my uncle's breast to arouse his flagging attention,—"while the Duchess, poor lady, was wandering amid the tempest in this disconsolate manner, she arrived at this chateau. Her approach caused some uneasiness; for the clattering of a troop of horse at dead of night up the avenue of a lonely chateau, in those unsettled times, and in a troubled part of the country, was enough to occasion alarm.

"A tall, broad-shouldered chasseur, armed to the teeth, galloped ahead, and announced the name of the visitor. All uneasiness was dispelled. The household turned out with flambeaux to receive her, and never did torches gleam on a more weather-beaten travel-stained band than came tramping into the court. Such pale, careworn faces, such bedraggled dresses, as the poor Duchess and her females presented, each seated behind her cavalier: while the half-drenched, half-drowsy pages and attendants seemed ready to fall from their horses with sleep and fatigue.

"The Duchess was received with a hearty welcome by my ancestor. She was ushered into the hall of the chateau, and the fires soon crackled and blazed, to cheer herself and her train; and every spit and stew-pan was put in requisition to prepare ample refreshment for the wayfarers.

"She had a right to our hospitalities," continued the Marquis, drawing himself up with a slight degree of stateliness, "for she was related to our family. I'll tell you how it was. Her father, Henry de Bourbon, Prince of Condé—"

"But did the Duchess pass the night in the chateau?" said my uncle rather abruptly, terrified at the idea of getting involved in one of the Marquis's genealogical discussions.

"Oh, as to the Duchess, she was put into the very apartment you occupied last night, which at that time was a kind of state-apartment. Her followers were quartered in the chambers opening upon the neighboring corridor, and her favorite page slept in an adjoining closet. Up and down the corridor walked the great chasseur who had announced her arrival, and who acted as a kind of sentinel or guard. He was a dark, stern, powerful-looking fellow; and as the light of a lamp in the corridor fell upon his deeply marked face and sinewy form, he seemed capable of defending the castle with his single arm.

"It was a rough, rude night; about this time of the year—apropos!—now I think of it, last night was the anniversary of her visit. I may well remember the precise date, for it was a night not to be forgotten by our house. There is a singular tradition concerning it in our family." Here the Marquis hesitated, and a cloud seemed to gather about his bushy eyebrows. "There is a tradition—that a strange occurrence took place that night.—A strange, mysterious, inexplicable occurrence—" Here he checked himself, and paused.

"Did it relate to that lady?" inquired my uncle, eagerly.

"It was past the hour of midnight," resumed the Marquis, —"when the whole chateau—" Here he paused again. My uncle made a movement of anxious curiosity.

"Excuse me," said the Marquis, a slight blush streaking

his sallow visage. "There are some circumstances connected with our family history which I do not like to relate. That was a rude period. A time of great crimes among great men: for you know high blood, when it runs wrong, will not run tamely, like blood of the *canaille*—poor lady!—But I have a little family pride, that—excuse me—we will change the subject, if you please—"

My uncle's curiosity was piqued. The pompous and magnificent introduction had led him to expect something wonderful in the story, to which it served as a kind of avenue. He had no idea of being cheated out of it by a sudden fit of unreasonable squeamishness. Besides, being a traveller in quest of information, he considered it his duty to inquire into everything.

The Marquis, however, evaded every question.

"Well," said my uncle, a little petulantly, "whatever you may think of it, I saw that lady last night."

The Marquis stepped back and gazed at him with surprise.

"She paid me a visit in my bedchamber."

The Marquis pulled out his snuff-box with a shrug and a smile; taking this no doubt for an awkward piece of English pleasantry, which politeness required him to be charmed with.

My uncle went on gravely, however, and related the whole circumstance. The Marquis heard him through with profound attention, holding his snuff-box unopened in his hand. When the story was finished, he tapped on the lid of his box deliberately, took a long, sonorous pinch of snuff—

"Bah!" said the Marquis, and walked towards the other end of the gallery.—

Here the narrator paused. The company waited for some time for him to resume his narration; but he continued silent.

"Well," said the inquisitive gentleman,—"and what did your uncle say then?"

"Nothing," replied the other.

"And what did the Marquis say farther?"

"Nothing."

"And is that all?"

"That is all," said the narrator, filling a glass of wine.

"I surmise," said the shrewd old gentleman with the waggish nose,—"I surmise the ghost must have been the old housekeeper, walking her rounds to see that all was right."

"Bah!" said the narrator. "My uncle was too much accustomed to strange sights not to know a ghost from a housekeeper."

There was a murmur round the table, half of merriment, half of disappointment. I was inclined to think the old gentleman had really an after-part of his story in reserve; but he sipped his wine and said nothing more; and there was an odd expression about his dilapidated countenance which left me in doubt whether he were in drollery or earnest.

"Egad," said the knowing gentleman, with the flexible nose, "this story of your uncle puts me in mind of one that used to be told of an aunt of mine, by the mother's side; though I don't know that it will bear a comparison, as the good lady was not so prone to meet with strange adventures. But at any rate you shall have it."

The Adventure of My Aunt

My aunt was a lady of large frame, strong mind, and great resolution: she was what might be termed a very manly woman. My uncle was a thin, puny little man, very meek and acquiescent, and no match for my aunt. It was observed that he dwindled and dwindled gradually away, from the day of his marriage. His wife's powerful mind was too much for him; it wore him out. My aunt, however, took all possible care of him: had half the doctors in town to prescribe for him; made him take all their prescriptions, and dosed him with physic enough to cure a whole hospital. All was in vain. My uncle grew worse and worse the more dosing and nursing he underwent, until in the end he added another to the long list of matrimonial victims who have been killed with kindness.

"And was it his ghost that appeared to her?" asked the inquisitive gentleman, who had questioned the former story-teller.

"You shall hear," replied the narrator.—My aunt took on mightily for the death of her poor dear husband. Perhaps she felt some compunction at having given him so much physic, and nursed him into the grave. At any rate, she did all that a widow could do to honor his memory. She spared no expense in either the quantity or quality of her mourning weeds; wore a miniature of him about her neck as large as a little sun-dial, and had a full-length portrait of him always hanging in her bed-chamber. All the world extolled her conduct to the skies; and it was determined that a woman who behaved so well to the memory of one husband deserved soon to get another.

It was not long after this that she went to take up her residence in an old country-seat in Derbyshire, which had long been in the care of merely a steward and housekeeper. She took most of her servants with her, intending to make it her principal abode. The house stood in a lonely wild part of the country, among the gray Derbyshire hills, with a murderer hanging in chains on a bleak height in full view.

The servants from town were half frightened out of their wits at the idea of living in such a dismal, pagan-looking place; especially when they got together in the servants' hall in the evening, and compared notes on all the hobgoblin stories picked up in the course of the day. They were afraid to venture alone about the gloomy, black-looking chambers. My lady's maid, who was troubled with nerves, declared she could never sleep alone in such a "gashly rummaging old building"; and the footman, who was a kind-hearted young fellow, did all in his power to cheer her up.

My aunt was struck with the lonely appearance of the house. Before going to bed, therefore, she examined well the fastnesses of the doors and windows; locked up the plate with her own hands, and carried the keys, together with a little box of money and jewels, to her own room; for she was a notable woman, and always saw to all things herself. Having put the keys under her pillow, and dismissed her maid, she sat by her toilet arranging her hair; for being, in spite of her grief for my uncle, rather a buxom widow, she was somewhat particular about her person. She sat for a little while looking at her face in the glass, first on one side then on the other, as ladies are apt to do when they would ascertain whether they have been in good looks; for a roistering country squire of the neighborhood, with whom she had flirted when a girl, had called that day to welcome her to the country.

All of a sudden she thought she heard something move behind her. She looked hastily round, but there was nothing to be seen. Nothing but the grimly painted portrait of her poor dear man, hanging against the wall.

She gave a heavy sigh to his memory, as she was accustomed to do whenever she spoke of him in company, and then went on adjusting her night-dress, and thinking of the squire. Her sigh was re-echoed, or answered by a long-drawn breath. She looked round again, but no one was to be seen. She ascribed these sounds to the wind oozing through the ratholes of the old mansion, and proceeded leisurely to put her hair in papers, when, all at once, she thought she perceived one of the eyes of the portrait move.

"The back of her head being towards it!" said the storyteller with the ruined head,—"good!"

"Yes, sir!" replied dryly the narrator, "her back being towards the portrait, but her eyes fixed on its reflection in the glass."—Well, as I was saying, she perceived one of the eyes of the portrait move. So strange a circumstance, as you may well suppose, gave her a sudden shock. To assure herself of the fact, she put one hand to her forehead as if rubbing it; peeped through her fingers, and moved the candle with the other hand. The light of the taper gleamed on the eye, and was reflected from it. She was sure it moved. Nay, more, it seemed to give her a wink, as she had sometimes known her husband to do when living! It struck a momentary chill to her heart; for she was a lone woman, and felt herself fearfully situated.

The chill was but transient. My aunt, who was almost as resolute a personage as your uncle, sir, (turning to the old story-teller,) became instantly calm and collected. She went on adjusting her dress. She even hummed an air, and did not make even a single false note. She casually overturned a dressing-box; took a candle and picked up the articles one by one from the floor, pursued a rolling pin-cushion that was making the best of its way under the bed; then opened the door; looked for an instant into the corridor, as if in doubt whether to go; and then walked quietly out.

She hastened down-stairs, ordered the servants to arm themselves with the weapons first at hand, placed herself at their head, and returned almost immediately.

Her hastily levied army presented a formidable force. The steward had a rusty blunder-buss, the coachman a loaded whip, the footman a pair of horse-pistols, the cook a huge chopping-knife, and the butler a bottle in each hand. My aunt led the van with a red-hot poker, and in my opinion she was the most formidable of the party. The waiting-maid, who dreaded to stay alone in the servants' hall, brought up the rear, smelling to a broken bottle of volatile salts, and expressing her terror of the ghostesses. "Ghosts!" said my aunt, resolutely. "I'll singe their whiskers for them!"

They entered the chamber. All was still and undisturbed as when she had left it. They approached the portrait of my uncle.

"Pull down that picture!" cried my aunt. A heavy groan, and a sound like the chattering of teeth, issued from the portrait. The servants shrunk back; the maid uttered a faint shriek, and clung to the footman for support.

"Instantly!" added my aunt, with a stamp of the foot.

The picture was pulled down, and from a recess behind it, in which had formerly stood a clock, they hauled forth a round-shouldered, black-bearded varlet, with a knife as long as my arm, but trembling all over like an aspen-leaf.

"Well, and who was he? No ghost, I suppose," said the inquisitive gentleman.

"A Knight of the Post," replied the narrator, "who had been smitten with the worth of the wealthy widow; or rather a marauding Tarquin, who had stolen into her chamber to violate her purse, and rifle her strong box, when all the house should be asleep. In plain terms," continued he, "the vagabond was a loose idle fellow of the neighborhood, who had once been a servant in the house, and had been employed to assist in arranging it for the reception of its mistress. He confessed that he had contrived this hiding-place for his nefarious purpose, and had borrowed an eye from the portrait by way of a reconnoitring-hole."

"And what did they do with him?—did they hang him?" resumed the questioner.

"Hang him!—how could they?" exclaimed a beetle-browed barrister, with a hawk's nose. "The offence was not capital. No robbery, no assault had been committed. No forcible entry or breaking into the premises—"

"My aunt," said the narrator, "was a woman of spirit, and apt to take the law in her own hands. She had her own notions of cleanliness also. She ordered the fellow to be drawn through the horse-pond, to cleanse away all offences, and then to be well rubbed down with an oaken towel."

"And what became of him afterwards?" said the inquisitive gentleman.

"I do not exactly know. I believe he was sent on a voyage of improvement to Botany Bay."

"And your aunt," said the inquisitive gentleman; "I'll warrant she took care to make her maid sleep in the room with her after that."

"No, Sir, she did better; she gave her hand shortly after to the roistering squire; for she used to observe, that it was a dismal thing for a woman to sleep alone in the country."

"She was right," observed the inquisitive gentleman, nodding sagaciously; "but I am sorry they did not hang that fellow."

It was agreed on all hands that the last narrator had brought his tale to the most satisfactory conclusion, though a country clergyman present regretted that the uncle and aunt, who figured in the different stories, had not been married together; they certainly would have been well matched.

"But I don't see, after all," said the inquisitive gentleman, "that there was any ghost in this last story."

"Oh! If it's ghosts you want, honey," cried the Irish Captain of Dragoons, "if it's ghosts you want, you shall have a whole regiment of them. And since these gentlemen have given the adventures of their uncles and aunts, faith, and I'll even give you a chapter out of my own family-history."

The Bold Dragoon

or The Adventure of My Grandfather

My grandfather was a bold dragoon, for it's a profession, d' ye see, that has run in the family. All my forefathers have been dragoons, and died on the field of honor, except myself, and I hope my posterity may be able to say the same; however, I don't mean to be vainglorious. Well, my grandfather, as I said, was a bold dragoon, and had served in the Low Countries. In fact, he was one of that very army, which according to my uncle Toby, swore so terribly in Flanders. He could swear a good stick himself; and moreover was the very man that introduced the doctrine Corporal Trim mentions of radical heat and radical moisture, or, in other words, the mode of keeping out the damps of ditchwater by burnt brandy. Be that as it may, it's nothing to the purport of my story. I only tell it to show you that my grandfather was a man not easily to be humbugged. He had seen service, or, according to his own phrase, he had seen the devil—and that's saying everything.

Well, gentlemen, my grandfather was on his way to England, for which he intended to embark from Ostend—bad luck to the place! for one where I was kept by storms and headwinds for three long days, and the devil of a jolly companion or pretty girl to comfort me. Well, as I was saying, my grandfather was on his way to England, or rather to Ostend—no matter which, it's all the same. So one evening, towards night fall, he rode jollily into Bruges.—Very like you all know Bruges, gentlemen; a queer old-fashioned Flemish town, once, they say, a great place for trade and money-making in old times, when the Mynheers were in their glory; but almost as large and as empty as an Irishman's pocket at the present day.—Well, gentlemen, it was at the time of the annual fair. All Bruges was crowded; and the canals swarmed with Dutch boats, and the streets swarmed with Dutch merchants; and there was hardly any getting along for goods, wares, and merchandises, and peasants in big breeches, and women in half a score of petticoats.

My grandfather rode jollily along, in his easy, slashing way, for he was a saucy, sun-shiny fellow—staring about him at the motley crowd, the old houses with gable ends to the street, and storks' nests in the chimneys; winking at the yafrows who showed their faces at the windows and joking with the women right and left in the street; all of whom laughed, and took it in amazing good part; for though he did not know a word of the language, yet he had always a knack of making himself understood among the women.

Well, gentlemen, it being the time of the annual fair, all the town was crowded, every inn and tavern full, and my grandfather applied in vain from one to the other for admittance. At length he rode up to an old rickety inn, that looked ready to fall to pieces, and which all the rats would have run away from, if they could have found room in any other house to put their heads. It was just such a queer building as you see in Dutch pictures, with a tall roof that reached up into the clouds, and as many garrets, one over the other, as the seven heavens of Mahomet. Nothing had saved it from tumbling down but a stork's nest on the chimney, which always brings good luck to a house in the Low Countries; and at the very time of my grandfather's arrival, there were two of these long-legged birds of grace standing like ghosts on the chimney-top. Faith, but they've kept the house on its legs to this very day, for you may see it any time you pass through Bruges, as it stands there yet, only it is turned into a brewery of strong Flemish beer,—at least it was so when I came that way after the battle of Waterloo.

My grandfather eyed the house curiously as he approached. It might not have altogether struck his fancy, had he not seen in large letters over the door,

HEER VERKOOPT MAN GOEDEN DRANK

My grandfather had learnt enough of the language to know that the sign promised good liquor. "This is the house for me," said he, stopping short before the door.

The sudden appearance of a dashing dragoon was an event in an old inn frequented only by the peaceful sons of traffic. A rich burgher of Antwerp, a stately ample man in a broad Flemish hat, and who was the great man and great patron of the establishment, sat smoking a clean long pipe on one side of the door; a fat little distiller of Geneva, from Schiedam, sat smoking on the other; and the bottle-nosed host stood in the door, and the comely hostess, in crimped cap, beside him; and the hostess's daughter, a plump Flanders lass, with long gold pendants in her ears, was at a side-window.

"Humph!" said the rich burgher of Antwerp, with a sulky glance at the stranger.

"De duyvel!" said the fat little distiller of Schiedam.

The landlord saw, with the quick glance of a publican, that the new guest was not at all to the taste of the old ones; and, to tell the truth, he did not like my grandfather's saucy eye. He shook his head. "Not a garret in the house but was full."

"Not a garret!" echoed the landlady.

"Not a garret!" echoed the daughter.

The burgher of Antwerp, and the little distiller of Schiedam, continued to smoke their pipes sullenly, eying the enemy askance from under their broad hats, but said nothing.

My grandfather was not a man to be browbeaten. He threw the reins on his horse's neck, cocked his head on one side, stuck one arm akimbo,—"Faith and troth!" said he, "but I'll sleep in this house this very night."—As he said this he gave a slap on his thigh, by way of emphasis—the slap went to the landlady's heart.

He followed up the vow by jumping off his horse, and making his way past the staring Mynheers into the public room.—Maybe you've been in the bar-room of an old Flemish inn—faith, but a handsome chamber it was as you'd wish to see; with a brick floor, and a great fireplace, with the whole Bible history in glazed tiles; and then the mantelpiece, pitching itself head foremost out of the wall, with a whole regiment of cracked tea-pots and earthen jugs paraded on it; not to mention half a dozen great Delft platters, hung about the room by way of pictures; and the little bar in one corner, and the bouncing bar-maid inside of it, with a red calico cap, and yellow ear-drops.

My grandfather snapped his fingers over his head, as he cast an eye round the room,—"Faith, this is the very house I've been looking after," said he.

There was some further show of resistance on the part of the garrison; but my grandfather was an old soldier, and an Irishman to boot, and not easily repulsed, especially after he had got into the fortress. So he blarneyed the landlord, kissed the landlord's wife, tickled the landlord's daughter, chucked the bar-maid under the chin; and it was agreed on all hands that it would be a thousand pities, and a burning shame into the bargain, to turn such a bold dragoon into the streets. So they laid their heads together, that is to say, my grandfather and the landlady, and it was at length agreed to accommodate him with an old chamber that had been for some time shut up.

"Some say it's haunted," whispered the landlord's daughter; "but you are a bold dragoon, and I dare say don't fear ghosts."

"The devil a bit!" said my grandfather, pinching her plump cheek. "But if I should be troubled by ghosts, I've been to the Red Sea in my time, and have a pleasant way of laying them, my darling."

And then he whispered something to the girl which made

her laugh, and give him a good-humored box on the ear. In short, there was nobody knew better how to make his way among the petticoats than my grandfather.

In a little while, as was his usual way, he took complete possession of the house, swaggering all over it; into the stable to look after his horse, into the kitchen to look after his supper. He had something to say or do with every one; smoked with the Dutchmen, drank with the Germans, slapped the landlord on the shoulder, romped with his daughter and the bar-maid;—never, since the days of Alley Croaker, had such a rattling blade been seen. The landlord stared at him with astonishment; the landlord's daughter hung her head and giggled whenever he came near; and as he swaggered along the corridor, with his sword trailing by his side, the maids looked after him, and whispered to one another, "What a proper man!"

At supper, my grandfather took command of the *table-d' hôte* as though he had been at home; helped everybody, not forgetting himself; talked with every one, whether he understood their language or not; and made his way into the intimacy of the rich burgher of Antwerp, who had never been known to be sociable with any one during his life. In fact, he revolutionized the whole establishment, and gave it such a rouse, that the very house reeled with it. He outsat every one at table, excepting the little fat distiller of Schiedam, who sat soaking a long time before he broke forth; but when he did, he was a very devil incarnate. He took a violent affection for my grandfather; so they sat drinking and smoking, and telling stories, and singing Dutch and Irish songs, without understanding a word each other said, until the little Hollander was fairly swamped with his own gin and water, and carried off to bed, whooping and hickuping and trolling the burden of a Low Dutch love-song.

Well, gentlemen, my grandfather was shown to his quarters up a large staircase, composed of loads of hewn timber; and through long rigmarole passages, hung with blackened paintings of fish, and fruit, and game, and country frolics, and huge kitchens, and portly burgomasters, such as you see about old-fashioned Flemish inns, till at length he arrived at his room.

An old-times chamber it was, sure enough, and crowded with all kinds of trumpery. It looked like an infirmary for decayed and superannuated furniture, where everything diseased or disabled was sent to nurse or to be forgotten. Or rather it might be taken for a general congress of old legitimate movables, where every kind and country had a representative. No two chairs were alike. Such high backs and low backs, and leather bottoms, and worsted bottoms, and straw bottoms, and no bottoms; and cracked marble tables with curiously carved legs, holding balls in their claws, as though they were going to play at nine-pins.

My grandfather made a bow to the motley assemblage as he entered, and, having undressed himself, placed his light in the fireplace, asking pardon of the tongs, which seemed to be making love to the shovel in the chimney-corner, and whispering soft nonsense in its ear.

The rest of the guests were by this time sound asleep, for your Mynheers are huge sleepers. The housemaids, one by one, crept up yawning to their attics; and not a female head in the inn was laid on a pillow that night without dreaming of the bold dragoon.

My grandfather, for his part, got into bed, and drew over him one of those great bags of down, under which they smother a man in the Low Countries; and there he lay, melting between two feather beds, like an anchovy sandwich between two slices of toast and butter. He was a warm-complexioned man, and this smothering played the very deuce with him. So, sure enough, in a little time it seemed as if a legion of imps were twitching at him, and all the blood in his veins was in a fever-heat.

He lay still however, until all the house was quiet excepting the snoring of the Mynheers from the different chambers; who answered one another in all kinds of tones and cadences, like so many bull-frogs in a swamp. The quieter the house became, the more unquiet became my grandfather. He waxed warmer and warmer, until at length the bed became too hot to hold him.

"Maybe the maid had warmed it too much?" said the curious gentleman, inquiringly.

"I rather think the contrary," replied the Irishman. "But, be that as it may, it grew too hot for my grandfather."

"Faith, there's no standing this any longer," says he. So he jumped out of bed, and went strolling about the house.

"What for?" said the inquisitive gentleman.

"Why, to cool himself, to be sure—or perhaps to find a more comfortable bed—or perhaps—But no matter what he went for—he never mentioned—and there's no use in taking up our time in conjecturing."

Well, my grandfather had been for some time absent from his room, and was returning, perfectly cool, when just as he reached the door, he heard a strange noise within. He paused and listened. It seemed as if some one were trying to hum a tune in defiance of the asthma. He recollected the report of the room being haunted; but he was no believer in ghosts, so he pushed the door gently open and peeped in.

Egad, gentlemen, there was a gambol carrying on within enough to have astonished St. Anthony himself. By the light of the fire he saw a pale weazen-faced fellow, in a long flannel gown and a tall white nightcap with a tassel to it, who sat by the fire with a bellows under his arm by way of bagpipe, from which he forced the asthmatical music that had bothered my grandfather. As he played, too, he kept twitching about with a thousand queer contortions, nodding his head, and bobbing about his tasselled night-cap.

My grandfather thought this very odd and mighty presumptuous, and was about to demand what business he had to play his wind-instrument in another gentleman's quarters, when a new cause of astonishment met his eye. From the opposite side of the room a long-backed, bandy-legged chair, covered with leather, and studded all over in a coxcombical fashion with little brass nails, got suddenly into motion, thrust out first a claw-foot, then a crooked arm, and at length, making a leg, sidled gracefully up to an easy-chair of tarnished brocade, with a hole in its bottom, and led it gallantly out in a ghostly minuet about the floor.

The musician now played fiercer and fiercer, and bobbed his head and his night-cap about like mad. By degrees the dancing mania seemed to seize upon all the other pieces of furniture. The antique, long-bodied chairs paired off in couples and led down a country-dance; a three-legged stool danced a hornpipe, though horribly puzzled by its supernumerary limb; while the amorous tongs seized the shovel round the waist, and whirled it about the room in a German waltz. In short, all the movables got in motion; pirouetting hands across, right and left, like so many devils; all except a great clothes-press, which kept courtesying and courtesying in a corner, like a dowager, in exquisite time to the music; being rather too corpulent to dance, or perhaps at a loss for a partner.

My grandfather concluded the latter to be the reason; so being, like a true Irishman, devoted to the sex, and at all times ready for a frolic, he bounced into the room, called to the musician to strike up Paddy O'Rafferty, capered up to the clothes-press, and seized upon the two handles to lead her out:—when-whirr! the whole revel was at an end. The chairs, tables, tongs and shovel, slunk in an instant as quietly into their places as if nothing had happened, and the musician vanished up the chimney, leaving the bellows behind him in his hurry. My grandfather found himself seated in the middle of the floor with the clothes-press sprawling before him, and the two handles jerked off, and in his hands.

"Then, after all, this was a mere dream," said the inquisitive gentleman.

"The divil a bit of a dream!" replied the Irishman. "There never was a truer fact in this world. Faith, I should have liked to see any man tell my grandfather it was a dream."

Well, gentlemen, as the clothes-press was a mighty heavy body, and my grandfather likewise, particularly in rear, you may easily suppose that two such heavy bodies coming to the ground would make a bit of a noise. Faith, the old mansion shook as though it had mistaken it for an earthquake. The whole garrison was alarmed. The landlord, who slept below, hurried up with a candle to inquire the cause, but with all his haste his daughter had arrived at the scene of uproar before him. The landlord was followed by the landlady, who was followed by the bouncing bar-maid, who was followed by the simpering chambermaids, all holding together, as well as they could, such garments as they first laid hands on; but all in a terrible hurry to see what the deuce was to pay in the chamber of the bold dragoon.

My grandfather related the marvellous scene he had witnessed, and the broken handles of the prostrate clothes-press bore testimony to the fact. There was no contesting such evidence; particularly with a lad of my grandfather's complexion, who seemed able to make good every word either with sword or shillelah. So the landlord scratched his head and looked silly, as he was apt to do when puzzled. The landlady scratched—no, she did not scratch her head, but she knit her brow, and did not seem half pleased with the explanation. But the landlady's daughter corroborated it by recollecting that the last person who had dwelt in that chamber was a famous juggler who died of St. Vitus's dance, and had no doubt infected all the furniture.

This set all things to rights, particularly when the chambermaids declared that they had all witnessed strange carryings on in that room; and as they declared this "upon their honors," there could not remain a doubt upon this subject.

"And did your grandfather go to bed again in that room?" said the inquisitive gentleman.

"That's more than I can tell. Where he passed the rest of the night was a secret he never disclosed. In fact, though he had seen much service, he was but indifferently acquainted with geography, and apt to make blunders in his travels about inns at night, which it would have puzzled him sadly to account for in the morning."

"Was he ever apt to walk in his sleep?" said the knowing old gentleman.

"Never that I heard of."

There was a little pause after this rigmarole Irish romance, when the old gentleman with the haunted head observed, that the stories hitherto related had rather a burlesque tendency. "I recollect an adventure however," added he, "which I heard of during a residence in Paris, for the truth of which I can undertake to vouch, and which is of a very grave and singular nature."

Adventure of the German Student

O n a stormy night, in the tempestuous times of the French revolution, a young German was returning to his lodgings, at a late hour, across the old part of Paris. The lightning gleamed, and the loud claps of thunder rattled through the lofty narrow streets—but I should first tell you something about this young German.

Gottfried Wolfgang was a young man of good family. He had studied for some time at Göttingen, but being of a visionary and enthusiastic character, he had wandered into those wild and speculative doctrines which have so often bewildered German students. His secluded life, his intense application and the singular nature of his studies, had an effect on both mind and body. His health was impaired; his imagination diseased. He had been indulging in fanciful speculations on spiritual essences, until, like Swedenborg, he had an ideal world of his own around him. He took up a notion, I do not know from what cause, that there was an evil influence hanging over him; an evil genius or spirit seeking to ensnare him and ensure his perdition. Such an idea working on his melancholy temperament, produced the most gloomy effects. He became haggard and desponding. His friends discovered the mental malady preying upon him, and determined that the best cure was a change of scene; he was sent, therefore, to finish his studies amidst the splendors and gayeties of Paris.

Wolfgang arrived at Paris at the breaking out of the revolution. The popular delirium at first caught his enthusiastic mind, and he was captivated by the political and philosophical theories of the day: but the scenes of blood which followed shocked his sensitive nature, disgusted him with society and the world, and made him more than ever a recluse. He shut himself up in a solitary apartment in the *Pays Latin,* the quarter of students. There, in a gloomy street not far from the monastic walls of the Sorbonne, he pursued his favorite speculations. Sometimes he spent hours together in the great libraries of Paris, those catacombs of departed authors, rummaging among their hordes of dusty and obsolete works in quest of food for his unhealthy appetite. He was, in a manner, a literary ghoul, feeding in the charnel-house of decayed literature.

Wolfgang, though solitary and reclusive, was of an ardent temperament, but for a time it operated merely upon his imagination. He was too shy and ignorant of the world to make any advances to the fair, but he was a passionate admirer of female beauty, and in his lonely chamber would often lose himself in reveries on forms and faces which he had seen, and his fancy would deck out images of loveliness far surpassing the reality.

While his mind was in this excited and sublimated state, a dream produced an extraordinary effect upon him. It was of a female face of transcendent beauty. So strong was the impression made, that he dreamt of it again and again. It haunted his thoughts by day, his slumbers by night; in fine, he became passionately enamoured of this shadow of a dream. This lasted so long that it became one of those fixed ideas which haunt the minds of melancholy men, and are at times mistaken for madness.

Such was Gottfried Wolfgang, and such his situation at the time I mentioned. He was returning home late one stormy night, through some of the old and gloomy streets of the *Marais*, the ancient part of Paris. The loud claps of thunder rattled among the high houses of the narrow streets. He came to the Place de Grève, the square where public executions are performed. The lightning quivered about the pinnacles of the ancient Hôtel de Ville, and shed flickering gleams over the open space in front. As Wolfgang was crossing the square, he shrank back with horror at finding himself close by the guillotine. It was the height of the reign of terror, when this dreadful instrument of death stood ever ready, and its scaffold was continually running with the blood of the virtuous and the brave. It had that very day been actively employed in the work of carnage, and there it stood in grim array, amidst a silent and sleeping city, waiting for fresh victims.

Wolfgang's heart sickened within him, and he was turning shuddering from the horrible engine, when he beheld a shadowy form, cowering as it were at the foot of the steps which led up to the scaffold. A succession of vivid flashes of lightning revealed it more distinctly. It was a female figure, dressed in black. She was seated on one of the lower steps of the scaffold, leaning forward, her face hid in her lap; and her long dishevelled tresses hanging to the ground, streaming with the rain which fell in torrents. Wolfgang paused. There was something awful in this solitary monument of woe. The female had the appearance of being above the common order. He knew the times to be full of vicissitude, and that many a fair head, which had once been pillowed on down, now wandered houseless. Perhaps this was some poor mourner whom the dreadful axe had rendered desolate, and who sat here heartbroken on the strand of existence, from which all that was dear to her had been launched into eternity.

He approached, and addressed her in the accents of sympathy. She raised her head and gazed wildly at him. What was his astonishment at beholding, by the bright glare of the lightning, the very face which had haunted him in his dreams. It was pale and disconsolate, but ravishingly beautiful.

Trembling with violent and conflicting emotions, Wolfgang again accosted her. He spoke something of her being exposed at such an hour of the night, and to the fury of such a storm, and offered to conduct her to her friends. She pointed to the guillotine with a gesture of dreadful signification.

"I have no friend on earth!" said she.

"But you have a home," said Wolfgang.

...and there it stood in grim array, amidst a silent and sleeping city, waiting for fresh victims.

"Yes—in the grave!"

The heart of the student melted at the words.

"If a stranger dare make an offer," said he, "without danger of being misunderstood, I would offer my humble dwelling as a shelter; myself as a devoted friend. I am friendless myself in Paris, and a stranger in the land; but if my life could be of service, it is at your disposal, and should be sacrificed before harm or indignity should come to you."

There was an honest earnestness in the young man's manner that had its effect. His foreign accent, too, was in his favor; it showed him not to be a hackneyed inhabitant of Paris. Indeed, there is an eloquence in true enthusiasm that is not to be doubted. The homeless stranger confided herself implicitly to the protection of the student.

He supported her faltering steps across the Pont Neuf, and by the place where the statue of Henry the Fourth had been overthrown by the populace. The storm had abated, and the thunder rumbled at a distance. All Paris was quiet; that great volcano of human passion slumbered for a while, to gather fresh strength for the next day's eruption. The student conducted his charge through the ancient streets of the *Pays Latin,* and by the dusky walls of the Sorbonne, to the great dingy hotel which he inhabited. The old portress who admitted them stared with surprise at the unusual sight of the melancholy Wolfgang with a female companion.

On entering his apartment, the student, for the first time, blushed at the scantiness and indifference of his dwelling. He had but one chamber—an old-fashioned saloon—heavily carved, and fantastically furnished with the remains of former magnificence, for it was one of those hotels in the quarter of the Luxembourg palace, which had once belonged to nobility. It was lumbered with books and papers, and all the usual apparatus of a student, and his bed stood in a recess at one end.

When lights were brought, and Wolfgang had a better opportunity of contemplating the stranger, he was more than ever intoxicated by her beauty. Her face was pale, but of a dazzling fairness, set off by a profusion of raven hair that hung clustering about it. Her eyes were large and brilliant, with a singular expression approaching almost to wildness. As far as her black dress permitted her shape to be seen, it was of perfect symmetry. Her whole appearance was highly striking, though she was dressed in the simplest style. The only thing approaching to an ornament which she wore, was a broad black band round her neck, clasped by diamonds.

The perplexity now commenced with the student how to dispose of the helpless being thus thrown upon his protection. He thought of abandoning his chamber to her, and seeking shelter for himself elsewhere. Still he was so fascinated by her charms, there seemed to be such a spell upon his thoughts and senses, that he could not tear himself from her presence. Her manner, too, was singular and unaccountable. She spoke no more of the guillotine. Her grief had abated. The attentions of the student had first won her confidence, and then, apparently, her heart. She was evidently an enthusiast like himself, and enthusiasts soon understand each other.

In the infatuation of the moment, Wolfgang avowed his

passion for her. He told her the story of his mysterious dream, and how she had possessed his heart before he had even seen her. She was strangely affected by his recital, and acknowledged to have felt an impulse towards him equally unaccountable. It was the time for wild theory and wild actions. Old prejudices and superstitions were done away; everything was under the sway of the "Goddess of Reason." Among other rubbish of the old times, the forms and ceremonies of marriage began to be considered superfluous bonds for honorable minds. Social compacts were the vogue. Wolfgang was too much of a theorist not to be tainted by the liberal doctrines of the day.

"Why should we separate?" said he; "our hearts are united; in the eye of reason and honor we are as one. What need is there of sordid forms to bind high souls together?"

The stranger listened with emotion: she had evidently received illumination at the same school.

"You have no home or family," continued he, "let me be everything to you, or rather let us be everything to one another. If form is necessary, form shall be observed—there is my hand. I pledge myself to you forever."

"Forever?" said the stranger, solemnly.

"Forever!" repeated Wolfgang.

The stranger clasped the hand extended to her: "Then I am yours," murmured she, and sank upon his bosom.

The next morning the student left his bride sleeping, and sallied forth at an early hour to seek more spacious apartments suitable to the change in his situation. When he returned, he found the stranger lying with her head hanging over the bed, and one arm thrown over it. He spoke to her, but received no reply. He advanced to awaken her from her uneasy posture. On taking her hand, it was cold—there was no pulsation—her face was pallid and ghastly. In a word, she was a corpse.

Horrified and frantic, he alarmed the house. A scene of confusion ensued. The police were summoned. As the officer of police entered the room, he started back on beholding the corpse.

"Great heaven!" cried he, "how did this woman come here?"

"Do you know anything about her?" said Wolfgang eagerly.

"Do I?" exclaimed the officer: "she was guillotined yesterday."

He stepped forward, undid the black collar round the neck of the corpse, and the head rolled on the floor!

The student burst into a frenzy. "The fiend! the fiend has gained possession of me!" shrieked he; "I am lost forever."

They tried to soothe him, but in vain. He was possessed with the frightful belief that an evil spirit had reanimated the dead body to ensnare him. He went distracted, and died in a mad-house.

Here the old gentleman with the haunted head finished his narrative.

"And is this really a fact?" said the inquisitive gentleman.

"A fact not to be doubted," replied the other. "I had it from the best authority. The student told it me himself. I saw him in a mad-house in Paris."

The Devil and Tom Walker

A few miles from Boston in Massachusetts, there is a deep inlet, winding several miles into the interior of the country from Charles Bay, and terminating in a thickly-wooded swamp or morass. On one side of this inlet is a beautiful dark grove; on the opposite side the land rises abruptly from the water's edge into a high ridge, on which grow a few scattered oaks of great age and immense size. Under one of these gigantic trees, according to old stories, there was a great amount of treasure buried by Kidd the pirate. The inlet allowed a facility to bring the money in a boat secretly and at night to the very foot of the hill; the elevation of the place permitted a good lookout to be kept that no one was at hand; while the remarkable trees formed good landmarks by which the place might easily be found again. The old stories add, moreover, that the devil presided at the hiding of the money, and took it under his guardianship; but this, it is well known, he always does with buried treasure, particularly when it has been ill-gotten. Be that as it may, Kidd never returned to recover his wealth;

being shortly after seized at Boston, sent out to England, and there hanged for a pirate.

About the year 1727, just at the time that earthquakes were prevalent in New England, and shook many tall sinners down upon their knees, there lived near this place a meagre, miserly fellow, of the name of Tom Walker. He had a wife as miserly as himself: they were so miserly that they even conspired to cheat each other. Whatever the woman could lay hands on, she hid away; a hen could not cackle but she was on the alert to secure the new-laid egg. Her husband was continually prying about to detect her secret hoards, and many and fierce were the conflicts that took place about what ought to have been common property. They lived in a forlorn-looking house that stood alone, and had an air of starvation. A few straggling savin-trees, emblems of sterility, grew near it; no smoke ever curled from its chimney; no traveller stopped at its door. A miserable horse, whose ribs were as articulate as the bars of a gridiron, stalked about a field, where a thin carpet of moss, scarcely covering the ragged beds of pudding-stone, tantalized and balked his hunger; and sometimes he would lean his head over the fence, look piteously at the passer-by, and seem to petition deliverance from this land of famine.

The house and its inmates had altogether a bad name. Tom's wife was a tall termagant, fierce of temper, loud of tongue, and strong of arm. Her voice was often heard in wordy warfare with her husband; and his face sometimes showed signs that their conflicts were not confined to words.

No one ventured, however, to interfere between them. The lonely wayfarer shrunk within himself at the horrid clamor and clapper-clawing; eyed the den of discord askance; and hurried on his way, rejoicing, if a bachelor, in his celibacy.

One day that Tom Walker had been to a distant part of the neighborhood, he took what he considered a short cut homeward, through the swamp. Like most short cuts, it was an illchosen route. The swamp was thickly grown with great gloomy pines and hemlocks, some of them ninety feet high, which made it dark at noonday, and a retreat for all the owls of the neighborhood. It was full of pits and quagmires, partly covered with weeds and mosses, where the green surface often betrayed the traveller into a gulf of black, smothering mud: there were also dark and stagnant pools, the abodes of the tadpole, the bull-frog, and the water-snake; where the trunks of pines and hemlocks lay half drowned, half rotting, looking like alligators sleeping in the mire.

Tom had long been picking his way cautiously through this treacherous forest; stepping from tuft to tuft of rushes and roots, which afforded precarious footholds among deep sloughs; or pacing carefully, like a cat, along the prostrate trunks of trees; startled now and then by the sudden screaming of the bittern, or the quacking of wild duck rising on the wing from some solitary pool. At length he arrived at a firm piece of ground, which ran out like a peninsula into the deep bosom of the swamp. It had been one of the strongholds of the Indians during their wars with the first colonists. Here they had thrown up a kind of fort, which they had looked upon as almost impregnable, and had used as a place of refuge for their squaws and children. Nothing remained of the old Indian fort but a few embankments, gradually sinking to the level of the surrounding earth, and already overgrown in part by oaks and other forest trees, the foliage of which formed a contrast to the dark pines and hemlocks of the swamp.

It was late in the dusk of evening when Tom Walker reached the old fort, and he paused there awhile to rest himself. Any one but he would have felt unwilling to linger in this lonely, melancholy place, for the common people had a bad opinion of it, from the stories handed down from the time of the Indian wars; when it was asserted that the savages held incantations here, and made sacrifices to the evil spirit.

Tom Walker, however, was not a man to be troubled with any fears of the kind. He reposed himself for some time on the trunk of a fallen hemlock, listening to the boding cry of the tree-toad, and delving with his walking-staff into a mound of black mould at his feet. As he turned up the soil unconsciously, his staff struck against something hard. He raked it out of the vegetable mould, and lo! a cloven skull, with an Indian tomahawk buried deep in it, lay before him. The rust on the weapon showed the time that had elapsed since this death-blow had been given. It was a dreary memento of the fierce struggle that had taken place in this last foothold of the Indian warriors.

"Humph!" said Tom Walker, as he gave it a kick to shake the dirt from it.

"Let that skull alone!" said a gruff voice. Tom lifted up his eyes, and beheld a great black man seated directly opposite him, on the stump of a tree. He was exceedingly surprised, having neither heard nor seen any one approach; and he was still more perplexed on observing, as well as the gathering gloom would permit, that the stranger was neither negro nor Indian. It is true he was dressed in a rude half Indian garb, and had a red belt or sash swathed round his body; but his face was neither black nor copper-color, but swarthy and dingy, and begrimed with soot, as if he had been accustomed to toil among fires and forges. He had a shock of coarse black hair, that stood out from his head in all directions, and bore an axe on his shoulder.

He scowled for a moment at Tom with a pair of great red eyes.

"What are you doing on my grounds?" said the black man, with a hoarse, growling voice.

"Your grounds!" said Tom, with a sneer, "no more your grounds than mine; they belong to Deacon Peabody."

"Deacon Peabody be d—d," said the stranger, "as I flatter myself he will be, if he does not look more to his own sins and less to those of his neighbors. Look yonder, and see how Deacon Peabody is faring."

Tom looked in the direction that the stranger pointed, and beheld one of the great trees, fair and flourishing without, but rotten at the core, and saw that it had been nearly hewn through, so that the first high wind was likely to blow it down. On the bark of the tree was scored the name of Deacon Peabody, an eminent man, who had waxed wealthy by driving shrewd bargains with the Indians. He now looked around, and found most of the tall trees marked with the name of some great man of the colony, and all more or less scored by the axe. The one on which he had been seated, and which had evidently just been hewn down, bore the name of Crowninshield; and he recollected a mighty rich man of that name, who made a vulgar display of wealth, which it was whispered he had acquired by buccaneering.

"He's just ready for burning!" said the black man, with a growl of triumph. "You see I am likely to have a good stock of firewood for winter."

"But what right have you," said Tom, "to cut down Deacon Peabody's timber?"

"The right of a prior claim," said the other. "This wood-land belonged to me long before one of your white-faced race put foot upon the soil."

"And pray, who are you, if I may be so bold?" said Tom.

"Oh, I go by various names. I am the wild huntsman in some countries; the black miner in others. In this neighbor-hood I am known by the name of the black woodsman. I am the great patron and prompter of slave-dealers, and the grand-master of the Salem witches."

"The upshot of all which is, that, if I mistake not," said Tom, sturdily, "you are he commonly called Old Scratch."

"The same, at your service!" replied the black man, with a half civil nod.

Such was the opening of this interview, according to the old story; though it has almost too familiar an air to be cred-ited. One would think that to meet with such a singular personage, in this wild, lonely place, would have shaken any man's nerves; but Tom was a hard-minded fellow, not easily daunted, and he had lived so long with a termagant wife, that he did not even fear the devil.

It is said that after this commencement they had a long and earnest conversation together, as Tom returned homeward. The black man told him of great sums of money buried by Kidd the pirate, under the oak-trees on the high ridge, not far from the morass. All these were under his command, and protected by his power, so that none could find them but such as propitiated his favor. These he offered to place within Tom Walker's reach, having conceived an especial kindness for him; but they were to be had only on certain conditions. What these conditions were may be easily surmised, though Tom never disclosed them publicly. They must have been very hard, for he required time to think of them, and he was not a man to stick at trifles when money was in view. When they had reached the edge of the swamp, the stranger paused. "What proof have I that all you have been telling me is true?" said Tom. "There's my signature," said the black man, pressing his finger on Tom's forehead. So saying, he turned off among the thickest of the swamp, and seemed, as Tom said, to go down, down, down, into the earth, until nothing but his head and shoulders could be seen, and so on, until he totally disappeared.

When Tom reached home, he found the black print of a finger burnt, as it were, into his forehead, which nothing could obliterate.

The first news his wife had to tell him was the sudden

death of Absalom Crowninshield, the rich buccaneer. It was announced in the papers with the usual flourish, that "A great man had fallen in Israel."

Tom recollected the tree which his black friend had just hewn down, and which was ready for burning. "Let the free-booter roast," said Tom; "who cares!" He now felt convinced that all he had heard and seen was no illusion.

He was not prone to let his wife into his confidence; but as this was an uneasy secret, he willingly shared it with her. All her avarice was awakened at the mention of hidden gold, and she urged her husband to comply with the black man's terms, and secure what would make them wealthy for life. However Tom might have felt disposed to sell himself to the devil, he was determined not to do so to oblige his wife; so he flatly refused, out of the mere spirit of contradiction. Many and bitter were the quarrels they had on the subject; but the more she talked, the more resolute was Tom not to be damned to please her.

At length she determined to drive the bargain on her own account, and if she succeeded, to keep all the gain to herself. Being of the same fearless temper as her husband, she set off for the old Indian fort towards the close of a summer's day. She was many hours absent. When she came back, she was reserved and sullen in her replies. She spoke something of a black man, whom she met about twilight hewing at the root of a tall tree. He was sulky, however, and would not come to terms: she was to go again with a propitiatory offering, but what it was she forbore to say.

The next evening she set off again for the swamp, with

her apron heavily laden. Tom waited and waited for her, but in vain; midnight came, but she did not make her appearance: morning, noon, night returned, but still she did not come. Tom now grew uneasy for her safety, especially as he found she had carried off in her apron the silver tea-pot and spoons, and every portable article of value. Another night elapsed, another morning came; but no wife. In a word, she was never heard of more.

What was her real fate nobody knows, in consequence of so many pretending to know. It is one of those facts which have become confounded by a variety of historians. Some asserted that she lost her way among the tangled mazes of the swamp, and sank into some pit or slough; others, more uncharitable, hinted that she had eloped with the household booty, and made off to some other province; while others surmised that the tempter had decoyed her into a dismal quagmire, on the top of which her hat was found lying. In confirmation of this, it was said a great black man, with an axe on his shoulder, was seen late that very evening coming out of the swamp, carrying a bundle tied in a check apron, with an air of surly triumph.

The most current and probable story, however, observes, that Tom Walker grew so anxious about the fate of his wife and his property, that he set out at length to seek them both at the Indian fort. During a long summer's afternoon he searched about the gloomy place, but no wife was to be seen. He called her name repeatedly, but she was nowhere to be heard. The bittern alone responded to his voice, as he flew screaming by; or the bull-frog croaked dolefully from a neighboring pool. At length, it is said, just in the brown hour of twilight, when the owls began to hoot, and the bats to flit about, his attention was attracted by the clamor of carrion crows hovering about a cypress-tree. He looked up, and beheld a bundle tied in a check apron, and hanging in the branches of the tree, with a great vulture perched hard by, as if keeping watch upon it. He leaped with joy; for he recognized his wife's apron, and supposed it to contain the household valuables.

"Let us get hold of the property," said he, consolingly to himself, "and we will endeavor to do without the woman."

As he scrambled up the tree, the vulture spread its wide wings, and sailed off screaming, into the deep shadows of the forest. Tom seized the checked apron, but, woful sight! found nothing but a heart and liver tied up in it!

Such, according to this most authentic old story, was all that was to be found of Tom's wife. She had probably attempted to deal with the black man as she had been accustomed to deal with her husband; but though a female scold is generally considered a match for the devil, yet in this instance she appears to have had the worst of it. She must have died game, however; for it is said Tom noticed many prints of cloven feet deeply stamped upon the tree, and found handfuls of hair, that looked as if they had been plucked from the coarse black shock of the woodman. Tom knew his wife's prowess by experience. He shrugged his shoulders, as he looked at the signs of a fierce clapper-clawing.

"Egad," said he to himself, "Old Scratch must have had a tough time of it!"

Tom consoled himself for the loss of his property, with the loss of his wife, for he was a man of fortitude. He even felt something like gratitude towards the black woodman, who, he considered, had done him a kindness. He sought, therefore, to cultivate a further acquaintance with him, but for some time without success; the old black-legs played shy, for whatever people may think, he is not always to be had for calling for: he knows how to play his cards when pretty sure of his game.

At length, it is said, when delay had whetted Tom's eagerness to the quick, and prepared him to agree to anything rather than not gain the promised treasure, he met the black man one evening in his usual woodman's dress, with his axe on his shoulder, sauntering along the swamp, and humming a tune. He affected to receive Tom's advances with great indifference, made brief replies, and went on humming his tune.

By degrees, however, Tom brought him to business, and they began to haggle about the terms on which the former was to have the pirate's treasure. There was one condition which need not be mentioned, being generally understood in all cases where the devil grants favors; but there were others about which, though of less importance, he was inflexibly obstinate. He insisted that the money found through his means should be employed in his service. He proposed, therefore, that Tom should employ it in the black traffic; that is to say, that he should fit out a slave-ship. This, however, Tom resolutely refused: he was bad enough in all conscience; but the devil himself could not tempt him to turn slave-trader.

Finding Tom so squeamish on this point, he did not insist upon it, but proposed, instead, that he should turn usurer; the devil being extremely anxious for the increase of usurers, looking upon them as his peculiar people.

To this no objections were made, for it was just to Tom's taste.

"You shall open a broker's shop in Boston next month," said the black man.

"I'll do it to-morrow, if you wish," said Tom Walker.

"You shall lend money at two per cent a month."

"Egad, I'll charge four!" replied Tom Walker.

"You shall extort bonds, foreclose mortgages, drive the merchants to bankruptcy"—

"I'll drive them to the d—l," cried Tom Walker.

"You are the usurer for my money!" said black-legs with delight. "When will you want the rhino?"

"This very night."

"Done!" said the devil.

"Done!" said Tom Walker,—So they shook hands and struck a bargain.

A few days' time saw Tom Walker seated behind his desk in a counting-house in Boston.

His reputation for a ready-moneyed man, who would lend money out for a good consideration, soon spread abroad. Everybody remembers the time of Governor Belcher,

He scowled for a moment at Tom with a pair of great red eyes.

when money was particularly scarce. It was a time of paper credit. The country had been deluged with government bills, the famous Land Bank had been established; there had been a rage for speculating; the people had run mad with schemes for new settlements; for building cities in the wilderness; land-jobbers went about with maps of grants, and townships, and Eldorados, lying nobody knew where, but which everybody was ready to purchase. In a word, the great speculating fever which breaks out every now and then in the country, had raged to an alarming degree, and everybody was dreaming of making sudden fortunes from nothing. As usual the fever had subsided; the dream had gone off, and the imaginary fortunes with it; the patients were left in doleful plight, and the whole country resounded with the consequent cry of "hard times."

At this propitious time of public distress did Tom Walker set up as usurer in Boston. His door was soon thronged by customers. The needy and adventurous; the gambling speculator, the dreaming land-jobber; the thriftless tradesman; the merchant with cracked credit; in short every one driven to raise money by desperate means and desperate sacrifices, hurried to Tom Walker.

Thus Tom was the universal friend of the needy, and acted like a "friend in need"; that is to say, he always exacted good pay and good security. In proportion to the distress of the applicant was the hardness of his terms. He accumulated bonds and mortgages; gradually squeezed his customers closer and closer: and sent them at length, dry as a sponge, from his door.

In this way he made money hand over hand; became a rich and mighty man, and exalted his cocked hat upon 'Change. He built himself, as usual, a vast house, out of ostentation; but left the greater part of it unfinished and unfurnished, out of parsimony. He even set up a carriage in the fulness of his vainglory, though he nearly starved the horses which drew it; and as the ungreased wheels groaned and screeched on the axle-trees, you would have thought you heard the souls of the poor debtors he was squeezing.

As Tom waxed old, however, he grew thoughtful. Having secured the good things of this world, he began to feel anxious about those of the next. He thought with regret on the bargain he had made with his black friend, and set his wits to work to cheat him out of the conditions. He became, therefore, all of a sudden, a violent church-goer. He prayed loudly and strenuously, as if heaven were to be taken by force of lungs. Indeed, one might always tell when he had sinned most during the week, by the clamor of his Sunday devotion. The quiet Christians who had been modestly and steadfastly travelling Zionward, were struck with self-reproach at seeing themselves so suddenly outstripped in their career by this new-made convert. Tom was as rigid in religious as in money matters; he was a stern supervisor and censurer of his neighbors, and seemed to think every sin entered up to their account became a credit on his own side of the page. He even talked of the expediency of reviving the persecution of Quakers and Anabaptists. In a word, Tom's zeal became as notorious as his riches.

Still, in spite of all this strenuous attention to forms, Tom had a lurking dread that the devil, after all, would have his due. That he might not be taken unawares, therefore, it is said he always carried a small Bible in his coat-pocket. He had also a great folio Bible on his counting-house desk, and would frequently be found reading it when people called on business; on such occasions he would lay his green spectacles in the book, to mark the place, while he turned round to drive some usurious bargain.

Some say that Tom grew a little crack-brained in his old days, and that, fancying his end approaching, he had his horse new shod, saddled and bridled, and buried with his feet uppermost; because he supposed that at the last day the world would be turned upside-down; in which case he should find his horse standing ready for mounting, and he was determined at the worst to give his old friend a run for it. This, however, is probably a mere-old wives' fable. If he really did take such a precaution, it was totally superfluous; at least so says the authentic old legend, which closes his story in the following manner:

One hot summer afternoon in the dog-days, just as a terrible black thunder gust was coming up, Tom sat in his counting-house, in his white cap and India silk morning-gown. He was on the point of foreclosing a mortgage, by which he would complete the ruin of an unlucky land-speculator for whom he had professed the greatest friendship. The poor land-jobber begged him to grant a few months' indulgence. Tom had grown testy and irritated, and refused another day.

"My family will be ruined and brought upon the parish,"

said the land-jobber. "Charity begins at home," replied Tom; "I must take care of myself in these hard times."

"You have made so much money out of me," said the speculator.

Tom lost his patience and his piety. "The devil take me," said he, "if I have made a farthing!"

Just then there were three loud knocks at the street door. He stepped out to see who was there. A black man was holding a black horse, which neighed and stamped with impatience.

"Tom, you're come for," said the black fellow, gruffly. Tom shrank back, but too late. He had left his little Bible at the bottom of his coat-pocket, and his big Bible on the desk buried under the mortgage he was about to foreclose: never was sinner taken more unawares. The black man whisked him like a child into the saddle, gave the horse the lash, and away he galloped, with Tom on his back, in the midst of the thunder-storm. The clerks stuck their pens behind their ears, and stared after him from the windows. Away went Tom Walker, dashing down the streets; his white cap bobbing up and down; his morning-gown fluttering in the wind, and his steed striking fire out of the pavement at every bound. When the clerks turned to look for the black man, he had disappeared.

Tom Walker never returned to foreclose the mortgage. A country-man, who lived on the border of the swamp, reported that in the height of the thunder-gust he had heard a great clattering of hoofs and a howling along the road, and running to the window caught sight of a figure, such as I have described, on a horse that galloped like mad across the fields, over the hills, and down into the black hemlock swamp towards the old Indian fort; and that shortly after a thunder-bolt falling in that direction seemed to set the whole forest in a blaze.

The good people of Boston shook their heads and shrugged their shoulders, but had been so much accustomed to witches and goblins, and tricks of the devil, in all kinds of shapes, from the first settlement of the colony, that they were not so much horror-struck as might have been expected. Trustees were appointed to take charge of Tom's effects. There was nothing, however, to administer upon. On search-ing his coffers, all his bonds and mortgages were found reduced to cinders. In place of gold and silver, his iron chest was filled with chips and shavings; two skeletons lay in his stable instead of his half-starved horses, and the very next day his great house took fire and burnt to the ground.

Such was the end of Tom Walker and his ill-gotten wealth. Let all griping money-brokers lay this story to heart. The truth of it is not to be doubted. The very hole under the oak-trees whence he dug Kidd's money is to be seen to this day; and the neighboring swamp and old Indian fort are often haunted in stormy nights by a figure on horseback, in morn-ing-gown and white cap, which is doubtless the troubled spirit of the usurer. In fact the story has resolved itself into a proverb, and is the origin of that popular saying, so prevalent throughout New England, of "The Devil and Tom Walker."

Legend of the Three
Beautiful Princesses

J n old times there reigned a Moorish king in Granada, whose name was Mohamed, to which his subjects added the appellation of El Hayzari, or "The Left-handed." Some say he was so called on account of his being really more expert with his sinister than his dexter hand; others, because he was prone to take everything by the wrong end, or, in other words, to mar wherever he meddled. Certain it is, either through misfortune or mismanagement, he was continually in trouble; thrice was he driven from his throne, and on one occasion barely escaped to Africa with his life, in the disguise of a fisherman. Still he was as brave as he was blundering; and though left-handed, wielded his scimitar to such purpose, that he each time re-established himself upon his throne by dint of hard fighting. Instead, however, of learning wisdom from adversity, he hardened his neck, and stiffened his left arm in wilfulness. The evils of a public nature which he thus brought upon himself and his kingdom may be learned by those who will delve into the Arabian annals of Granada; the present legend deals but with his domestic policy.

As this Mohamed was one day riding forth with a train of his courtiers, by the foot of the mountain of Elvira, he met a band of horsemen returning from a foray into the land of the Christians. They were conducting a long string of mules laden with spoil, and many captives of both sexes, among whom the monarch was struck with the appearance of a beautiful damsel, richly attired, who sat weeping on a low palfrey, and heeded not the consoling words of a *duenna* who rode beside her.

The monarch was struck with her beauty, and, on inquiring of the captain of the troop, found that she was the daughter of the Alcalde of a frontier fortress, that had been surprised and sacked in the course of the foray. Mohamed claimed her as his royal share of the booty, and had her conveyed to his harem in the Alhambra. There everything was devised to soothe her melancholy; and the monarch, more and more enamored, sought to make her his queen. The Spanish maid at first repulsed his addresses; he was an infidel; he was the open foe of her country; what was worse, he was stricken in years!

The monarch, finding his assiduities of no avail, determined to enlist in his favor the *duenna*, who had been captured with the lady. She was an Andalusian by birth, whose Christian name is forgotten, being mentioned in Moorish legends by no other appellation than that of the discreet Kadiga; and discreet in truth she was, as her whole history makes evident. No sooner had the Moorish king held a little private conversation with her, than she saw at once the cogency of his reasoning, and undertook his cause with her young mistress.

"Go to, now!" cried she; "what is there in all this to weep and wail about? Is it not better to be mistress of this beautiful palace, with all its gardens and fountains, than to be shut up within your father's old frontier tower? As to this Mohamed being an infidel, what is that to the purpose? You marry him, not his religion; and if he is waxing a little old, the sooner will you be a widow, and mistress of yourself; at any rate, you are in his power, and must either be a queen or a slave. When in the hands of a robber, it is better to sell one's merchandise for a fair price, than to have it taken by main force."

The arguments of the discreet Kadiga prevailed. The Spanish lady dried her tears, and became the spouse of Mohamed the Left-handed; she even conformed, in appearance, to the faith of her royal husband; and her discreet *duenna* immediately became a zealous convert to the Moslem doctrines: it was then the latter received the Arabian name of Kadiga, and was permitted to remain in the confidential employ of her mistress.

In due process of time the Moorish king was made the proud and happy father of three lovely daughters, all born at a birth; he could have wished they had been sons, but consoled himself with the idea that three daughters at a birth were pretty well for a man somewhat stricken in years, and left-handed!

As usual with all Moslem monarchs, he summoned his astrologers on this happy event. They cast the nativities of the three princesses, and shook their heads. "Daughters, O king!" said they, "are always precarious property; but these will most need your watchfulness when they arrive at a marriageable age; at that time gather them under your wings, and trust them to no other guardianship."

Mohamed the Left-handed was acknowledged to be a wise king by his courtiers, and was certainly so considered by himself. The prediction of the astrologers caused him but little disquiet, trusting to his ingenuity to guard his daughters and outwit the Fates.

The threefold birth was the last matrimonial trophy of the monarch; his queen bore him no more children, and died within a few years, bequeathing her infant daughters to his love, and to the fidelity of the discreet Kadiga.

Many years had yet to elapse before the princesses would arrive at that period of danger—the marriageable age. "It is good, however, to be cautious in time," said the shrewd monarch; so he determined to have them reared in the royal castle of Salobreña. This was a sumptuous palace, incrusted, as it were, in a powerful Moorish fortress on the summit of a hill overlooking the Mediterranean Sea. It was a royal retreat, in which the Moslem monarchs shut up such of their relatives as might endanger their safety; allowing them all kinds of luxuries and amusements, in the midst of which they passed their lives in voluptuous indolence.

Here the princesses remained, immured from the world, but surrounded by enjoyment, and attended by female slaves who anticipated their wishes. They had delightful gardens for their recreation, filled with the rarest fruits and flowers, with aromatic groves and perfumed baths. On three sides the castle looked down upon a rich valley, enamelled with all kinds of culture, and bounded by the lofty Alpuxarra mountains; on the other side it overlooked the broad sunny sea.

In this delicious abode, in a propitious climate, and under a cloudless sky, the three princesses grew up into wondrous beauty; but though all reared alike, they gave early tokens of diversity of character. Their names were Zayda, Zorayda, and Zorahayda; and such was their order of seniority, for there had been precisely three minutes between their births.

Zayda, the eldest, was of an intrepid spirit, and took the lead of her sisters in everything, as she had done in entering into the world. She was curious and inquisitive, and fond of getting at the bottom of things.

Zorayda had a great feeling for beauty, which was the reason, no doubt, of her delighting to regard her own image in a mirror or a fountain, and of her fondness for flowers, and jewels, and other tasteful ornaments.

As to Zorahayda, the youngest, she was soft and timid, and extremely sensitive, with a vast deal of disposable tenderness, as was evident from her number of pet-flowers, and pet-birds, and pet-animals, all of which she cherished with the fondest care. Her amusements, too, were of a gentle nature, and mixed up with musing and reverie. She would sit for hours in a balcony, gazing on the sparkling stars of a summer's night, or on the sea when lit up by the moon; and at such times, the song of a fisherman, faintly heard from the beach, or the notes of a Moorish flute from some gliding bark, sufficed to elevate her feelings into ecstasy. The least uproar of the elements, however, filled her with dismay; and a clap of thunder was enough to throw her into a swoon.

Years rolled on smoothly and serenely; the discreet Kadiga, to whom the princesses were confided, was faithful to her trust, and attended them with unremitting care.

The castle of Salobreña, as has been said, was built upon a hill on the sea-coast. One of the exterior walls straggled down the profile of the hill, until it reached a jutting rock over-hanging the sea, with a narrow sandy beach at its foot, laved by the rippling billows. A small watch-tower on this rock had been fitted up as a pavilion, with latticed windows to admit the sea-breeze. Here the princesses used to pass the sultry hours of mid-day.

The curious Zayda was one day seated at a window of the pavilion, as her sisters, reclining on ottomans, were taking the siesta or noontide slumber. Her attention was attracted to a galley which came coasting along, with measured strokes of the oar. As it drew near, she observed that it was filled with armed men. The galley anchored at the foot of the tower. A number of Moorish soldiers landed on the narrow beach, conducting several Christian prisoners. The curious Zayda awakened her sisters, and all three peeped cautiously through the close jalousies of the lattice which screened them from sight. Among the prisoners were three Spanish cavaliers, richly dressed. They were in the flower of youth, and of noble presence; and the lofty manner in which they carried themselves, though loaded with chains and surrounded with enemies, bespoke the grandeur of their souls. The princesses gazed with intense and breathless interest. Cooped up as they had been in this castle among female attendants, seeing nothing of the male sex but slaves, or the rude fishermen of the sea-coast, it is not to be wondered at that the appearance of three gallant cavaliers, in the pride of youth and manly beauty, should produce some commotion in their bosom.

"Did ever nobler being tread the earth than that cavalier in crimson?" cried Zayda, the eldest of the sisters. "See how proudly he bears himself, as though all around him were his slaves!"

"But notice that one in green!" exclaimed Zorayda. "What grace! what elegance! what spirit!"

The gentle Zorahayda said nothing, but she secretly gave preference to the cavalier in blue.

The princesses remained gazing until the prisoners were out of sight; then, heaving long-drawn sighs, they turned round, looked at each other for a moment, and sat down, musing and pensive, on their ottomans.

The discreet Kadiga found them in this situation. They related what they had seen; and even the withered heart of the *duenna* was warmed. "Poor youths!" exclaimed she, "I'll warrant their captivity makes many a fair and high-born lady's heart ache in their native land! Ah! my children, you have little idea of the life these cavaliers lead in their own country. Such prankling at tournaments! such devotion to the ladies! such courting and serenading!"

The curiosity of Zayda was fully aroused; she was insatiable in her inquiries, and drew from the *duenna* the most animated pictures of the scenes of her youthful days and native land. The beautiful Zorayda bridled up, and slyly regarded herself in a mirror, when the theme turned upon the charms of the Spanish ladies; while Zorahayda suppressed a struggling sigh at the mention of moonlight serenades.

Every day the curious Zayda renewed her inquiries, and every day the sage *duenna* repeated her stories, which were listened to with profound interest, though with frequent sighs, by her gentle auditors. The discreet old woman awoke at length to the mischief she might be doing. She had been accustomed to think of the princesses only as children; but they had imperceptibly ripened beneath her eye, and now bloomed before her three lovely damsels of the marriageable age. It is time, thought the *duenna*, to give notice to the king.

Mohamed the Left-handed was seated one morning on a divan in a cool hall of the Alhambra, when a slave arrived from the fortress of Salobreña, with a message from the sage Kadiga, congratulating him on the anniversary of his daughters' birthday. The slave at the same time presented a delicate little basket, decorated with flowers, within which, on a couch of vine and fig-leaves, lay a peach, an apricot, and a nectarine, with their bloom and down and dewy sweetness upon them, and all in the early stage of tempting ripeness. The monarch was versed in the Oriental language of fruits and flowers, and rapidly divined the meaning of this emblematical offering.

"So," said he, "the critical period pointed out by the astrologers is arrived: my daughters are at a marriageable age. What is to be done? They are shut up from the eyes of men; they are under the eyes of the discreet Kadiga—all very

good; but still they are not under my own eye, as was prescribed by the astrologers. I must gather them under my
wing, and trust to no other guardianship."

So saying, he ordered that a tower of the Alhambra
should be prepared for their reception, and departed at the
head of his guards for the fortress of Salobreña, to conduct
them home in person.

About three years had elapsed since Mohamed had
beheld his daughters, and he could scarcely credit his eyes at
the wonderful change which that small space of time had
made in their appearance. During the interval, they had
passed that wondrous boundary line in female life which
separates the crude, unformed, and thoughtless girl from the
blooming, blushing, meditative woman. It is like passing
from the flat, bleak, uninteresting plains of La Mancha to the
voluptuous valleys and swelling hills of Andalusia.

Zayda was tall and finely formed, with a lofty demeanor
and a penetrating eye. She entered with a stately and decided step, and made a profound reverence to Mohamed, treating him more as her sovereign than her father. Zorayda was
of the middle height, with an alluring look and swimming
gait, and a sparkling beauty, heightened by the assistance of
the toilette. She approached her father with a smile, kissed
his hand, and saluted him with several stanzas from a popular Arabian poet, with which the monarch was delighted.
Zorahayda was shy and timid, smaller than her sisters, and
with a beauty of that tender, beseeching kind which looks for
fondness and protection. She was little fitted to command,
like her elder sister, or to dazzle, like the second, but was

rather formed to creep to the bosom of manly affection, to nestle within it, and be content. She drew near to her father, with a timid and almost faltering step, and would have taken his hand to kiss; but on looking up into his face, and seeing it beaming with a paternal smile, the tenderness of her nature broke forth, and she threw herself upon his neck.

Mohamed the Left-handed surveyed his blooming daughters with mingled pride and perplexity, for while he exulted in their charms, he bethought himself of the prediction of the astrologers. "Three daughters! three daughters!" muttered he repeatedly to himself, "and all of a marriageable age! Here's tempting Hesperian fruit, that requires a dragon watch!"

He prepared for his return to Granada, by sending heralds before him, commanding every one to keep out of the road by which he was to pass, and that all doors and windows should be closed at the approach of the princesses. This done, he set forth, escorted by a troop of black horsemen of hideous aspect, and clad in shining armor.

The princesses rode beside the king, closely veiled, on beautiful white palfreys, with velvet caparisons, embroidered with gold, and sweeping the ground; the bits and stirrups were of gold, and the silken bridles adorned with pearls and precious stones. The palfreys were covered with little silver bells, which made the most musical tinkling as they ambled gently along. Woe to the unlucky wight, however, who lingered in the way when he heard the tinkling of these bells!—the guards were ordered to cut him down without mercy.

Legend of the Three Beautiful Princesses

The cavalcade was drawing near to Granada, when it overtook, on the banks of the river Xenil, a small body of Moorish soldiers with a convoy of prisoners. It was too late for the soldiers to get out of the way, so they threw themselves on their faces on the earth, ordering their captives to do the like. Among the prisoners were the three identical cavaliers whom the princesses had seen from the pavilion. They either did not understand, or were too haughty to obey the order, and remained standing and gazing upon the cavalcade as it approached.

The ire of the monarch was kindled at this flagrant defiance of his orders. Drawing his scimitar, and pressing forward, he was about to deal a left-handed blow that might have been fatal to at least one of the gazers, when the princesses crowded round him, and implored mercy for the prisoners; even the timid Zorahayda forgot her shyness, and became eloquent in their behalf. Mohamed paused, with uplifted scimitar, when the captain of the guard threw himself at his feet. "Let not your highness," said he, "do a deed that may cause great scandal throughout the kingdom. These are three brave and noble Spanish knights, who have been taken in battle, fighting like lions; they are of high birth, and may bring great ransoms." "Enough!" said the king. "I will spare their lives, but punish their audacity—let them be taken to the Vermilion Towers, and put to hard labor."

Mohamed was making one of his usual left-handed blunders. In the tumult and agitation of this blustering scene, the veils of the three princesses had been thrown back, and the radiance of their beauty revealed; and in prolonging the parley, the king had given that beauty time to have its full effect. In those days people fell in love much more suddenly than at present, as all ancient stories make manifest. It is not a matter of wonder, therefore, that the hearts of the three cavaliers were completely captured; especially as gratitude was added to their admiration. It is a little singular, however, though no less certain, that each of them was enraptured with a several beauty. As to the princesses, they were more than ever struck with the noble demeanor of the captives, and cherished in their breasts all that they had heard of their valor and noble lineage.

The cavalcade resumed its march; the three princesses rode pensively along on their tinkling palfreys, now and then stealing a glance behind in search of the Christian captives, and the latter were conducted to their allotted prison in the Vermilion Towers.

The residence provided for the princesses was one of the most dainty that fancy could devise. It was in a tower somewhat apart from the main palace of the Alhambra, though connected with it by the wall which encircled the whole summit of the hill. On one side it looked into the interior of the fortress, and had, at its foot, a small garden filled with the rarest flowers. On the other side it overlooked a deep embowered ravine separating the grounds of the Alhambra from those of the Generalife. The interior of the tower was divided into small fairy apartments, beautifully ornamented in the light Arabian style, surrounding a lofty hall, the vaulted roof of which rose almost to the summit of the tower. The walls and ceilings of the hall were adorned with arabesque and fretwork, sparkling with gold and with brilliant pen-cilling. In the centre of the marble pavement was an alabaster fountain, set round with aromatic shrubs and flowers, and throwing up a jet of water that cooled the whole edifice and had a lulling sound. Round the hall were suspended cages of gold and silver wire, containing singing birds of the finest plumage or sweetest note.

The princesses had been represented as always cheerful when in the castle of the Salobreña; the king had expected to see them enraptured with the Alhambra. To his surprise, however, they began to pine, and grow melancholy, and dissatisfied with everything around them. The flowers yield-ed them no fragrance, the song of the nightingale disturbed their night's rest, and they were out of all patience with the alabaster fountain, with its eternal drop-drop and splash-splash, from morning till night and from night till morning.

The king, who was somewhat of a testy, tyrannical dispo-sition, took this at first in high dudgeon; but he reflected that his daughters had arrived at an age when the female mind expands and its desires augment. "They are no longer chil-dren," said he to himself, "they are women grown, and require suitable objects to interest them." He put in requisi-tion, therefore, all the dressmakers, and the jewellers, and the artificers in gold and silver throughout the Zacatin of Granada, and the princesses were overwhelmed with robes of silk, and tissue, and brocade, and cashmere shawls, and necklaces of pearls and diamonds, and rings, and bracelets, and anklets, and all manner of precious things.

All, however, was of no avail; the princesses continued pale and languid in the midst of their finery, and looked like three blighted rosebuds, drooping from one stalk. The king was at his wits' end. He had in general a laudable confidence in his own judgment, and never took advice. "The whims and caprices of three marriageable damsels, however, are sufficient," said he, "to puzzle the shrewdest head." So for once in his life he called in the aid of counsel.

The person to whom he applied was the experienced *duenna*.

"Kadiga," said the king, "I know you to be one of the most discreet women in the whole world, as well as one of the most trustworthy; for these reasons I have always continued you about the persons of my daughters. Fathers cannot be too wary in whom they repose such confidence; I now wish you to find out the secret malady that is preying upon the princesses, and to devise some means of restoring them to health and cheerfulness."

Kadiga promised implicit obedience. In fact she knew more of the malady of the princesses than they themselves. Shutting herself up with them, however, she endeavored to insinuate herself into their confidence.

"My dear children, what is the reason you are so dismal and downcast in so beautiful a place, where you have everything that heart can wish?"

The princesses looked vacantly round the apartment, and sighed.

"What more, then, would you have? Shall I get you the

wonderful parrot that talks all languages, and is the delight of Granada?"

"Odious!" exclaimed the princess Zayda. "A horrid, screaming bird, that chatters words without ideas: one must be without brains to tolerate such a pest."

"Shall I send for a monkey from the rock of Gibraltar, to divert you with his antics?"

"A monkey! faugh!" cried Zorayda; "the detestable mimic of man. I hate the nauseous animal."

"What say you to the famous black singer Casem, from the royal harem, in Morocco? They say he has a voice as fine as a woman's."

"I have lost all relish for music," said the delicate Zorahayda.

"Ah! my child, you would not say so," replied the old woman, slyly, "had you heard the music I heard last evening, from the three Spanish cavaliers whom we met on our journey. But bless me, children! what is the matter that you blush so and are in such a flutter?"

"Nothing, nothing, good mother; pray proceed."

"Well; as I was passing by the Vermilion Towers last evening, I saw the three cavaliers resting after their day's labor. One was playing on the guitar, so gracefully, and the others sang by turns; and they did it in such style, that the very guards seemed like statues, or men enchanted. Allah forgive me! I could not help being moved at hearing the songs of my native country. And then to see three such noble and handsome youths in chains and slavery!"

Here the kind-hearted old woman could not restrain her tears.

"Perhaps, mother, you could manage to procure us a sight of these cavaliers," said Zayda.

"I think," said Zorayda, "a little music would be quite reviving."

The timid Zorahayda said nothing, but threw her arms round the neck of Kadiga.

"Mercy on me!" exclaimed the discreet old woman, "what are you talking of, my children? Your father would be the death of us all if he heard of such a thing. To be sure, these cavaliers are evidently well-bred and high-minded youths; but what of that? They are the enemies of our faith, and you must not even think of them but with abhorrence."

There is an admirable intrepidity in the female will, particularly when about the marriageable age, which is not to be deterred by dangers and prohibitions. The princesses hung round their old *duenna*, and coaxed, and entreated, and declared that a refusal would break their hearts.

What could she do? She was certainly the most discreet old woman in the whole world, and one of the most faithful servants to the king; but was she to see three beautiful princesses break their hearts for the mere tinkling of a guitar? Besides, though she had been so long among the Moors, and changed her faith in imitation of her mistress, like a trusty follower, yet she was a Spaniard born, and had the lingerings of Christianity in her heart. So she set about to contrive how the wish of the princesses might be gratified.

The Christian captives, confined in the Vermilion Towers,

were under the charge of a big-whiskered, broad-shouldered *renegado*, called Hussein Baba, who was reputed to have a most itching palm. She went to him privately, and slipping a broad piece of gold into his hand, "Hussein Baba," said she, "my mistresses the three princesses, who are shut up in the tower, and in sad want of amusement, have heard of the musical talents of the three Spanish cavaliers, and are desirous of hearing a specimen of their skill. I am sure you are too kind-hearted to refuse them so innocent a gratification."

"What! and to have my head set grinning over the gate of my own tower! for that would be the reward, if the king should discover it."

"No danger of anything of the kind; the affair may be managed so that the whim of the princesses may be gratified, and their father be never the wiser. You know the deep ravine outside of the walls which passes immediately below the tower. Put the three Christians to work there, and at the intervals of their labor, let them play and sing, as if for their own recreation. In this way the princesses will be able to hear them from the windows of the tower, and you may be sure of their paying well for your compliance."

As the good old woman concluded her harangue, she kindly pressed the rough hand of the *renegado*, and left within it another piece of gold.

Her eloquence was irresistible. The very next day the three cavaliers were put to work in the ravine. During the noontide heat, when their fellow-laborers were sleeping in the shade, and the guard nodding drowsily at his post, they seated themselves among the herbage at the foot of the tower, and sang a Spanish roundelay to the accompaniment of the guitar.

The glen was deep, the tower was high, but their voices rose distinctly in the stillness of the summer noon. The princesses listened from their balcony; they had been taught the Spanish language by their *duenna,* and were moved by the tenderness of the song. The discreet Kadiga, on the contrary, was terribly shocked. "Allah preserve us!" cried she, "they are singing a love-ditty, addressed to yourselves. Did ever mortal hear of such audacity? I will run to the slave-master, and have them soundly bastinadoed."

"What! bastinado such gallant cavaliers, and for singing so charmingly!" The three beautiful princesses were filled with horror at the idea. With all her virtuous indignation, the good old woman was of a placable nature, and easily appeased. Besides, the music seemed to have a beneficial effect upon her young mistresses. A rosy bloom had already come to their cheeks, and their eyes began to sparkle. She made no further objection, therefore, to the amorous ditty of the cavaliers.

When it was finished, the princesses remained silent for a time; at length Zorayda took up a lute, and with a sweet, though faint and trembling voice, warbled a little Arabian air, the burden of which was, "The rose is concealed among her leaves, but she listens with delight to the song of the nightingale."

From this time forward the cavaliers worked almost daily in the ravine. The considerate Hussein Baba became more and more indulgent, and daily more prone to sleep at his post. For some time a vague intercourse was kept up by popular songs and romances, which in some measure responded to each other, and breathed the feelings of the parties. By degrees the princesses showed themselves at the balcony, when they could do so without being perceived by the guards. They conversed with the cavaliers also, by means of flowers, with the symbolical language of which they were mutually acquainted; the difficulties of their intercourse added to its charms, and strengthened the passion they had so singularly conceived; for love delights to struggle with difficulties, and thrives the most hardily on the scantiest soil.

The change effected in the looks and spirits of the princesses by this secret intercourse, surprised and gratified the left-handed king; but no one was more elated than the discreet Kadiga, who considered it all owing to her able management.

At length there was an interruption in this telegraphic correspondence; for several days the cavaliers ceased to make their appearance in the glen. The princesses looked out from the tower in vain. In vain they stretched their swan-like necks from the balcony; in vain they sang like captive nightingales in their cage: nothing was to be seen of their Christian lovers; not a note responded from the groves. The discreet Kadiga sallied forth in quest of intelligence, and soon returned with a face full of trouble. "Ah, my children!" cried she, "I saw what all this would come to, but you would have your way; you may now hang up your lutes on the willows. The Spanish cavaliers are ransomed by their families;

they are down in Granada, and preparing to return to their native country."

The three beautiful princesses were in despair at the tidings. Zayda was indignant at the slight put upon them, in thus being deserted without a parting word. Zorayda wrung her hands and cried, and looked in the glass, and wiped away her tears, and cried afresh. The gentle Zorahayda leaned over the balcony and wept in silence, and her tears fell drop by drop among the flowers of the bank, where the faithless cavaliers had so often been seated.

The discreet Kadiga did all in her power to soothe their sorrow. "Take comfort, my children," said she, "this is nothing when you are used to it. This is the way of the world. Ah! when you are as old as I am, you will know how to value these men. I'll warrant these cavaliers have their loves among the Spanish beauties of Cordova and Seville, and will soon be serenading under their balconies, and thinking no more of the Moorish beauties in the Alhambra. Take comfort, therefore, my children, and drive them from your hearts."

The comforting words of the discreet Kadiga only redoubled the distress of the three princesses, and for two days they continued inconsolable. On the morning of the third the good old woman entered their apartment, all ruffling with indignation.

"Who would have believed such insolence in mortal man!" exclaimed she, as soon as she could find words to express herself; "but I am rightly served for having connived at this deception of your worthy father. Never talk more to me of your Spanish cavaliers."

"Why, what has happened, good Kadiga?" exclaimed the princesses in breathless anxiety.

"What has happened?—treason has happened! or, what is almost as bad, treason has been proposed; and to me, the most faithful of subjects, the trustiest of *duennas*! Yes, my children, the Spanish cavaliers have dared to tamper with me, that I should persuade you to fly with them to Cordova, and become their wives!"

Here the excellent old woman covered her face with her hands, and gave way to a violent burst of grief and indignation. The three beautiful princesses turned pale and red, pale and red, and trembled, and looked down, and cast shy looks at each other, but said nothing. Meantime the old woman sat rocking backward and forward in violent agitation, and now and then breaking out into exclamations: "That ever I should live to be so insulted!—I, the most faithful of servants!"

At length the eldest princess, who had most spirit and always took the lead, approached her, and laying her hand upon her shoulder, "Well, mother," said she, "supposing we were willing to fly with these Christian cavaliers—is such a thing possible?"

The good old woman paused suddenly in her grief, looking up, "Possible," echoed she; "to be sure it is possible. Have not the cavaliers already bribed Hussein Baba, the *renegado* captain of the guard, and arranged the whole plan? But then, to think of deceiving your father! your father, who has placed such confidence in me!" Here the worthy woman gave way to a fresh burst of grief, and began again to rock backward and forward, and to wring her hands.

"But our father has never placed any confidence in us," said the eldest princess, "but has trusted to bolts and bars, and treated us as captives."

"Why, that is true enough," replied the old woman, again pausing in her grief; "he has indeed treated you most unreasonably, keeping you shut up here, to waste your bloom in a moping old tower, like roses left to wither in a flower-jar. But, then, to fly from your native land!"

"And is not the land we fly to the native land of our mother, where we shall live in freedom? And shall we not each have a youthful husband in exchange for a severe old father?"

"Why, that again is all very true; and your father, I must confess, is rather tyrannical; but what then," relapsing into her grief, "would you leave me behind to bear the brunt of his vengeance?"

"By no means, my good Kadiga; cannot you fly with us?"

"Very true, my child; and to tell the truth, when I talked the matter over with Hussein Baba, he promised to take care of me, if I would accompany you in your flight; but then, bethink you, my children, are you willing to renounce the faith of your father?"

"The Christian faith was the original faith of our mother," said the eldest princess; "I am ready to embrace it, and so, I am sure, are my sisters."

"Right again," exclaimed the old woman, brightening up; "it was the original faith of your mother, and bitterly did she lament on her deathbed that she had renounced it. I promised her then to take care of your souls, and I rejoice to see that they are now in a fair way to be saved. Yes, my children, I too was born a Christian, and have remained a Christian in my heart, and am resolved to return to the faith. I have talked on the subject with Hussein Baba, who is a Spaniard by birth, and comes from a place not far from my native town. He is equally anxious to see his own country, and to be reconciled to the Church; and the cavaliers have promised that, if we are disposed to become man and wife, on returning to our native land, they will provide for us handsomely."

In a word, it appeared that this extremely discreet and provident old woman had consulted with the cavaliers and the *renegado*, and had concerted the whole plan of escape. The eldest princess immediately assented to it, and her example, as usual, determined the conduct of her sisters. It is true, the youngest hesitated, for she was gentle and timid of soul, and there was a struggle in her bosom between filial feeling and youthful passion; the latter, however, as usual, gained the victory, and with silent tears and stifled sighs she prepared herself for flight.

The rugged hill on which the Alhambra is built was, in old times, perforated with subterranean passages cut through the rock and leading from the fortress to various parts of the city and to distant sally-ports on the banks of the Darro and the Xenil. They had been constructed at different times by the Moorish kings as means of escape from sudden insurrections, or of secretly issuing forth on private enterprises. Many of them are now entirely lost, while others remain, partly choked with rubbish, and partly walled up, —

monuments of the jealous precautions and warlike strata-
gems of the Moorish government. By one of these passages
Hussein Baba had undertaken to conduct the princesses to a
sally-port beyond the walls of the city, where the cavaliers
were to be ready with fleet steeds, to bear the whole party
over the borders.

The appointed night arrived; the tower of the princesses
had been locked up as usual, and the Alhambra was buried
in deep sleep. Towards midnight the discreet Kadiga listened
from the balcony of a window that looked into the garden.
Hussein Baba, the *renegado*, was already below, and gave the
appointed signal. The *duenna* fastened the end of a ladder of
ropes to the balcony, lowered it into the garden and descended. The two eldest princesses followed her with beating
hearts; but when it came to the turn of the youngest princess,
Zorahayda, she hesitated and trembled. Several times she
ventured a delicate little foot upon the ladder, and as often
drew it back, while her poor little heart fluttered more and
more the longer she delayed. She cast a wistful look back into
the silken chamber; she had lived in it, to be sure, like a bird
in a cage; but within it she was secure; who could tell what
dangers might beset her should she flutter forth into the
wide world! Now she bethought her of her gallant Christian
lover, and her little foot was instantly upon the ladder; and
anon she thought of her father, and shrank back. But fruitless
is the attempt to describe the conflict in the bosom of one so
young and tender and loving, but so timid and so ignorant of
the world.

In vain her sisters implored, the *duenna* scolded, and the

renegado blasphemed beneath the balcony: the gentle little Moorish maid stood doubting and wavering on the verge of elopement; tempted by the sweetness of the sin, but terrified at its perils.

Every moment increased the danger of discovery. A distant tramp was heard. "The patrols are walking their rounds," cried the *renegado*; "if we linger, we perish. Princess, descend instantly, or we leave you."

Zorahayda was for a moment in fearful agitation; then loosening the ladder of ropes, with desperate resolution she flung it from the balcony.

"It is decided!" cried she; "flight is now out of my power! Allah guide and bless ye, my dear sisters!"

The two eldest princesses were shocked at the thought of leaving her behind, and would fain have lingered, but the patrol was advancing; the *renegado* was furious, and they were hurried away to the subterraneous passage. They groped their way through a fearful labyrinth, cut through the heart of the mountain, and succeeded in reaching, undiscovered, an iron gate that opened outside of the walls. The Spanish cavaliers were waiting to receive them, disguised as Moorish soldiers of the guard, commanded by the *renegado*.

The lover of Zorahayda was frantic when he learned that she had refused to leave the tower; but there was no time to waste in lamentations. The two princesses were placed behind their lovers, the discreet Kadiga mounted behind the *renegado*, and they all set off at a round pace in the direction of the Pass of Lope, which leads through the mountains towards Cordova.

They had not proceeded far when they heard the noise of drums and trumpets from the battlements of the Alhambra.

"Our flight is discovered!" said the *renegado*.

"We have fleet steeds, the night is dark, and we may distance all pursuit," replied the cavaliers.

They put spurs to their horses, and scoured across the Vega. They attained the foot of the mountain of Elvira, which stretches like a promontory into the plain. The *renegado* paused and listened. "As yet," said he, "there is no one on our traces, we shall make good our escape to the mountains." While he spoke, a light blaze sprang up on the top of the watch-tower of the Alhambra.

"Confusion!" cried the *renegado*, "that bale fire will put all the guards of the passes on the alert. Away! away! Spur like mad,—there is no time to be lost."

Away they dashed—the clattering of their horses' hoofs echoed from rock to rock, as they swept along the road that skirts the rocky mountain of Elvira. As they galloped on, the bale fire of the Alhambra was answered in every direction; light after light blazed on the *atalayas*, or watch-towers of the mountains.

"Forward! forward!" cried the *renegado*, with many an oath, "to the bridge,—to the bridge, before the alarm has reached there!"

They doubled the promontory of the mountains, and arrived in sight of the famous Bridge of Pinos, that crosses a rushing stream often dyed with Christian and Moslem blood. To their confusion, the tower on the bridge blazed with lights and glittered with armed men. The *renegado* pulled up his steed, rose in his stirrups, and looked about him for a moment; then beckoning to the cavaliers, he struck off from the road, skirted the river for some distance, and dashed into its waters. The cavaliers called upon the princesses to cling to them, and did the same. They were borne for some distance down the rapid current, the surges roared round them, but the beautiful princesses clung to their Christian knights, and never uttered a complaint. The cavaliers attained the opposite bank in safety, and were conducted by the *renegado*, by rude and unfrequented paths and wild *barrancos*, through the heart of the mountains, so as to avoid all the regular passes. In a word, they succeeded in reaching the ancient city of Cordova; where their restoration to their country and friends was celebrated with great rejoicings, for they were of the noblest families. The beautiful princesses were forthwith received into the bosom of the Church, and, after being in all due form made regular Christians, were rendered happy wives.

In our hurry to make good the escape of the princesses across the river, and up the mountains, we forgot to mention the fate of the discreet Kadiga. She had clung like a cat to Hussein Baba in the scamper across the Vega, screaming at every bound, and drawing many an oath from the whiskered *renegado*; but when he prepared to plunge his steed into the river, her terror knew no bounds. "Grasp me not so tightly," cried Hussein Baba; "hold on by my belt and fear nothing." She held firmly with both hands by the leathern belt that girded the broad-backed *renegado*; but when he halted with the cavaliers to take breath on the mountain summit, the *duenna* was no longer to be seen.

"What has become of Kadiga?" cried the princesses in alarm.

"Allah alone knows!" replied the *renegado*, "my belt came loose when in the midst of the river, and Kadiga was swept with it down the stream. The will of Allah be done! but it was an embroidered belt, and of great price."

There was no time to waste in idle regrets; yet bitterly did the princesses bewail the loss of their discreet counsellor. That excellent old woman, however, did not lose more than half of her nine lives in the water; a fisherman, who was drawing his nets some distance down the stream, brought her to land, and was not a little astonished at his miraculous draught. What further became of the discreet Kadiga, the legend does not mention; certain it is that she evinced her discretion in never venturing within the reach of Mohamed the Left-handed.

Almost as little is known of the conduct of that sagacious monarch when he discovered the escape of his daughters, and the deceit practised upon him by the most faithful of servants. It was the only instance in which he had called in the aid of counsel, and he was never afterwards known to be guilty of a similar weakness. He took good care, however, to guard his remaining daughter, who had no disposition to elope; it is thought, indeed, that she secretly repented having remained behind: now and then she was seen leaning on the battlements of the tower, and looking mournfully towards the mountains in the direction of Cordova, and sometimes the notes of her lute were heard accompanying plaintive ditties, in which she was said to lament the loss of her sisters and her lover, and to bewail her solitary life. She died young, and, according to popular rumor, was buried in a vault beneath the tower, and her untimely fate has given rise to more than one traditionary fable.

The following legend, which seems in some measure to spring out of the foregoing story, is too closely connected with high historic names to be entirely doubted. The Count's daughter, and some of her young companions, to whom it was read in one of the evening *tertullias*, thought certain parts of it had much appearance of reality; and Dolores, who was much more versed than they in the improbable truths of the Alhambra, believed every word of it.

Legend of the Rose
of the Alhambra

For some time after the surrender of Granada by the Moors, that delightful city was a frequent and favorite residence of the Spanish sovereigns, until they were frightened away by successive shocks of earthquakes, which toppled down various houses, and made the old Moslem towers rock to their foundation.

Many, many years then rolled away, during which Granada was rarely honored by a royal guest. The palaces of the nobility remained silent and shut up; and the Alhambra, like a slighted beauty, sat in mournful desolation among her neglected gardens. The Tower of the Infantas, once the residence of the three beautiful Moorish princesses, partook of the general desolation; the spider spun her web athwart the gilded vault, and bats and owls nestled in those chambers that had been graced by the presence of Zayda, Zorayda, and Zorahayda. The neglect of this tower may have been partly owing to some superstitious notions of the neighbors. It was rumored that the spirit of the youthful Zorahayda, who had perished in that tower, was often seen by moonlight seated beside the fountain in the hall, or moaning about the battlements, and that the notes of her silver lute would be heard at midnight by wayfarers passing along the glen.

At length the city of Granada was once more welcomed by the royal presence. All the world knows that Philip V was the first Bourbon that swayed the Spanish sceptre. All the world knows that he married, in second nuptials, Elizabetta or Isabella (for they are the same), the beautiful princess of Parma; and all the world knows that by this chain of contingencies a French prince and an Italian princess were seated together on the Spanish throne. For a visit of this illustrious pair, the Alhambra was repaired and fitted up with all possible expedition. The arrival of the court changed the whole aspect of the lately deserted palace. The clangor of drum and trumpet, the tramp of steed about the avenues and outer court, the glitter of arms and display of banners about barbican and battlement, recalled the ancient and war-like glories of the fortress. A softer spirit, however, reigned within the royal palace. There was the rustling of robes and the cautious tread and murmuring voice of reverential courtiers about the ante-chambers, a loitering of pages and maids of honor about the gardens, and the sound of music stealing from open casements.

Among those who attended in the train of the monarchs was a favorite page of the queen, named Ruyz de Alarcon. To say that he was a favorite page of the queen was at once to speak his eulogium, for every one in the suite of the stately

Elizabetta was chosen for grace, and beauty, and accomplishments. He was just turned of eighteen, light and lithe of form, and graceful as a young Antinous. To the queen he was all deference and respect, yet he was at heart a roguish stripling, petted and spoiled by the ladies about the court, and experienced in the ways of women far beyond his years.

This loitering page was one morning rambling about the groves of the Generalife, which overlook the grounds of the Alhambra. He had taken with him for his amusement a favorite gerfalcon of the queen. In the course of his rambles, seeing a bird rising from a thicket, he unhooded the hawk and let him fly. The falcon towered high in the air, made a swoop at his quarry, but missing it, soared away, regardless of the calls of the page. The latter followed the truant bird with his eye, in its capricious flight, until he saw it alight upon the battlements of a remote and lonely tower, in the outer wall of the Alhambra, built on the edge of a ravine that separated the royal fortress from the grounds of the Generalife. It was in fact the "Tower of the Princesses."

The page descended into the ravine and approached the tower, but it had no entrance from the glen, and its lofty height rendered any attempt to scale it fruitless. Seeking one of the gates of the fortress, therefore, he made a wide circuit to that side of the tower facing within the walls.

A small garden, enclosed by a trellis-work of reeds overhung with myrtle, lay before the tower. Opening a wicket, the page passed between beds of flowers and thickets of roses to the door. It was closed and bolted. A crevice in the door gave him a peep into the interior. There was a small Moorish hall with fretted walls, light marble columns, and an alabaster fountain surrounded with flowers. In the centre hung a gilt cage containing a singing-bird; beneath it, on a chair, lay a tortoise-shell cat among reels of silk and other articles of female labor, and a guitar decorated with ribbons leaned against the fountain.

Ruyz de Alarcon was struck with these traces of female taste and elegance in a lonely and, as he had supposed, deserted tower. They reminded him of the tales of enchanted halls current in the Alhambra; and the tortoise-shell cat might be some spell-bound princess.

He knocked gently at the door. A beautiful face peeped out from a little window above, but was instantly withdrawn. He waited, expecting that the door would be opened, but he waited in vain; no footstep was to be heard within— all was silent. Had his senses deceived him, or was this beautiful apparition the fairy of the tower? He knocked again, and more loudly. After a little while the beaming face once more peeped forth; it was that of a blooming damsel of fifteen.

The page immediately doffed his plumed bonnet, and entreated in the most courteous accents to be permitted to ascend the tower in pursuit of his falcon.

"I dare not open the door, Señor," replied the little damsel, blushing, "my aunt has forbidden it." "I do beseech you, fair maid—it is the favorite falcon of the queen. I dare not return to the palace without it."

"Are you then one of the cavaliers of the court?"

"I am, fair maid; but I shall lose the queen's favor and my place, if I lose this hawk."

"*Santa Maria*! It is against you cavaliers of the court my aunt has charged me especially to bar the door."

"Against wicked cavaliers doubtless, but I am none of these, but a simple, harmless page, who will be ruined and undone if you deny me this small request."

The heart of the little damsel was touched by the distress of the page. It was a thousand pities he should be ruined for the want of so trifling a boon. Surely too he could not be one of those dangerous beings whom her aunt had described as a species of cannibal, ever on the prowl to make prey of thoughtless damsels; he was gentle and modest, and stood so entreatingly with cap in hand, and looked so charming.

The sly page saw that the garrison began to waver, and redoubled his entreaties in such moving terms that it was not in the nature of mortal maiden to deny him; so the blushing little warden of the tower descended, and opened the door with a trembling hand, and if the page had been charmed by a mere glimpse of her countenance from the window, he was ravished by the full-length portrait now revealed to him.

Her Andalusian bodice and trim *basquiña* set off the round but delicate symmetry of her form, which was as yet scarce verging into womanhood. Her glossy hair was parted on her forehead with scrupulous exactness, and decorated with a fresh-plucked rose according to the universal custom of the country. It is true her complexion was tinged by the ardor of a southern sun, but it served to give richness to the mantling bloom of her cheek, and to heighten the lustre of her melting eyes.

Ruyz de Alarcon beheld all this with a single glance, for it became him not to tarry; he merely murmured his acknowledgments, and then bounded lightly up the spiral staircase in quest of his falcon.

He soon returned with the truant bird upon his fist. The damsel, in the meantime, had seated herself by the fountain in the hall, and was winding silk; but in her agitation she let fall the reel upon the pavement. The page sprang and picked it up, then dropping gracefully on one knee, presented it to her; but, seizing the hand extended to receive it, imprinted on it a kiss more fervent and devout than he had ever imprinted on the fair hand of his sovereign.

"Ave Maria, Señor!" exclaimed the damsel, blushing still deeper with confusion and surprise, for never before had she received such a salutation.

The modest page made a thousand apologies, assuring her it was the way at court of expressing the most profound homage and respect.

Her anger, if anger she felt, was easily pacified, but her agitation and embarrassment continued, and she sat blushing deeper and deeper, with her eyes cast down upon her work, entangling the silk which she attempted to wind.

The cunning page saw the confusion in the opposite camp, and would fain have profited by it, but the fine speeches he would have uttered died upon his lips; his attempts at gallantry were awkward and ineffectual; and to his surprise, the adroit page, who had figured with such grace and effrontery among the most knowing and experienced ladies of the court, found himself awed and abased in the presence of a simple damsel of fifteen.

In fact, the artless maiden, in her own modesty and innocence, had guardians more effectual than the bolts and bars prescribed by her vigilant aunt. Still, where is the female bosom proof against the first whisperings of love? The little damsel, with all her artlessness, instinctively comprehended all that the faltering tongue of the page failed to express, and her heart was fluttered at beholding, for the first time, a lover at her feet—and such a lover!

The diffidence of the page, though genuine, was short-lived, and he was recovering his usual ease and confidence, when a shrill voice was heard at a distance.

"My aunt is returning from mass!" cried the damsel in affright; "I pray you, Señor, depart."

"Not until you grant me that rose from your hair as a remembrance."

She hastily untwisted the rose from her raven locks. "Take it," cried she, agitated and blushing, "but pray begone."

The page took the rose, and at the same time covered with kisses the fair hand that gave it. Then, placing the flower in his bonnet, and taking the falcon upon his fist, he bounded off through the garden, bearing away with him the heart of the gentle Jacinta.

When the vigilant aunt arrived at the tower, she remarked

the agitation of her niece, and an air of confusion in the hall; but a word of explanation sufficed. "A gerfalcon had pursued his prey into the hall."

"Mercy on us! to think of a falcon flying into the tower. Did ever one hear of so saucy a hawk? Why, the very bird in the cage is not safe!"

The vigilant Fredegonda was one of the most wary of ancient spinsters. She had a becoming terror and distrust of what she denominated "the opposite sex," which had gradually increased through a long life of celibacy. Not that the good lady had ever suffered from their wiles, nature having set up a safeguard in her face that forbade all trespass upon her premises; but ladies who have least cause to fear for themselves are most ready to keep a watch over their more tempting neighbors.

The niece was the orphan of an officer who had fallen in the wars. She had been educated in a convent, and had recently been transferred from her sacred asylum to the immediate guardianship of her aunt, under whose overshadowing care she vegetated in obscurity, like an opening rose blooming beneath a brier. Nor indeed is this comparison entirely accidental; for, to tell the truth, her fresh and dawning beauty had caught the public eye, even in her seclusion, and, with that poetical turn common to the people of Andalusia, the peasantry of the neighborhood had given her the appellation of "the Rose of the Alhambra."

The wary aunt continued to keep a faithful watch over her tempting little niece as long as the court continued at Granada, and flattered herself that her vigilance had been successful. It is true the good lady was now and then dis-composed by the tinkling of guitars and chanting of love-dit-ties from the moonlit groves beneath the tower; but she would exhort her niece to shut her ears against such idle minstrelsy, assuring her that it was one of the arts of the opposite sex, by which simple maids were often lured to their undoing. Alas! what chance with a simple maid has a dry lecture against a moonlight serenade?

At length King Philip cut short his sojourn at Granada, and suddenly departed with all his train. The vigilant Fredegonda watched the royal pageant as it issued forth from the Gate of Justice and descended the great avenue leading to the city. When the last banner disappeared from her sight, she returned exulting to her tower, for all her cares were over. To her surprise, a light Arabian steed pawed the ground at the wicket-gate of the garden;—to her horror she saw through the thickets of roses a youth in gayly embroi-dered dress, at the feet of her niece. At the sounds of her foot-steps he gave a tender adieu, bounded lightly over the barri-er of reeds and myrtles, sprang upon his horse, and was out of sight in an instant.

The tender Jacinta, in the agony of her grief, lost all thought of her aunt's displeasure. Throwing herself into her arms, she broke forth into sobs and tears.

"*Ay de mi!*" cried she; "he's gone! he's gone! and I shall never see him more!"

"Gone!—who is gone?—what youth is that I saw at your feet?"

"A queen's page, aunt, who came to bid me farewell."

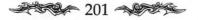

"A queen's page, child!" echoed the vigilant Fredegonda, faintly, "and when did you become acquainted with the queen's page?"

"The morning that the gerfalcon came into the tower. It was the queen's gerfalcon, and he came in pursuit of it."

"Ah silly, silly girl! know that there are no gerfalcons half so dangerous as these young prankling pages, and it is precisely such simple birds as thee that they pounce upon."

The aunt was at first indignant at learning that in despite of her boasted vigilance, a tender intercourse had been carried on by the youthful lovers, almost beneath her eye; but when she found that her simple-hearted niece, though thus exposed, without the protection of bolt or bar, to all the machinations of the opposite sex, had come forth unsinged from the fiery ordeal, she consoled herself with the persuasion that it was owing to the chaste and cautious maxims in which she had, as it were, steeped her to the very lips.

While the aunt laid this soothing unction to her pride, the niece treasured up the oft-repeated vows of fidelity of the page. But what is the love of restless, roving man? A vagrant stream that dallies for a time with each flower upon its bank, then passes on, and leaves them all in tears.

Days, weeks, months, elapsed, and nothing more was heard of the page. The pomegranate ripened, the vine yielded up its fruit, the autumnal rains descended in torrents from the mountains; the Sierra Nevada became covered with a snowy mantle, and wintry blasts howled through the halls of the Alhambra—still he came not. The winter passed away.

Again the genial spring burst forth with song and blossom and balmy zephyr; the snows melted from the mountains, until none remained but on the lofty summit of Nevada, glistening through the sultry summer air. Sill nothing was heard of the forgetful page.

In the meantime the poor little Jacinta grew pale and thoughtful. Her former occupations and amusements were abandoned, her silk lay entangled, her guitar unstrung, her flowers were neglected, the notes of her bird unheeded, and her eyes, once so bright, were dimmed with secret weeping. If any solitude could be devised to foster the passion of a love-lorn damsel it would be such a place as the Alhambra, where everything seems disposed to produce tender and romantic reveries. It is a very paradise for lovers; how hard then to be alone in such a paradise—and not merely alone, but forsaken!

"Alas, silly child!" would the staid and immaculate Fredegonda say, when she found her niece in one of her desponding moods—"did I not warn thee against the wiles and deceptions of these men? What couldst thou expect, too, from one of a haughty and aspiring family—thou an orphan, the descendant of a fallen and impoverished line? Be assured, if the youth were true, his father, who is one of the proudest nobles about the court, would prohibit his union with one so humble and portionless as thou. Pluck up thy resolution therefore, and drive these idle notions from thy mind."

The words of the immaculate Fredegonda only served to

increase the melancholy of her niece, but she sought to indulge it in private. At a late hour one midsummer night, after her aunt had retired to rest, she remained alone in the hall of the tower, seated beside the alabaster fountain. It was here that the faithless page had first knelt and kissed her hand; it was here that he had often vowed eternal fidelity. The poor little damsel's heart was overladen with sad and tender recollections, her tears began to flow, and slowly fell drop by drop into the fountain. By degrees the crystal water became agitated, and—bubble—bubble—bubble—boiled up and was tossed about, until a female figure, richly clad in Moorish robes, slowly rose to view.

Jacinta was so frightened that she fled from the hall and did not venture to return. The next morning she related what she had seen to her aunt, but the good lady treated it as a fantasy of her troubled mind, or supposed she had fallen asleep and dreamt beside the fountain. "Thou hast been thinking of the story of the three Moorish princesses that once inhabited this tower," continued she, "and it has entered into thy dreams."

"What story, aunt? I know nothing of it."

"Thou hast certainly heard of the three princesses, Zayda, Zorayda, and Zorahayda, who were confined in this tower by the king their father, and agreed to fly with three Christian cavaliers. The two first accomplished their escape, but the third failed in her resolution, and, it is said, died in this tower."

"I now recollect to have heard of it," said Jacinta, "and to have wept over the fate of the gentle Zorahayda."

"Thou mayest well weep over her fate," continued the aunt, "for the lover of Zorahayda was thy ancestor. He long bemoaned his Moorish love; but time cured him of his grief, and he married a Spanish lady, from whom thou art descended."

Jacinta ruminated over these words. "That which I have seen is no fantasy of the brain," said she to herself, "I am confident. If indeed it be the spirit of the gentle Zorahayda, which I have heard lingers about this tower, of what should I be afraid? I'll watch by the fountain tonight—perhaps the visit will be repeated."

Towards midnight, when everything was quiet, she again took her seat in the hall. As the bell in the distant watch-tower of the Alhambra struck the midnight hour, the fountain was again agitated; and bubble—bubble—bubble—it tossed about the waters until the Moorish female again rose to view. She was young and beautiful; her dress was rich with jewels, and in her hand she held a silver lute. Jacinta trembled and was faint, but was reassured by the soft and plaintive voice of the apparition, and the sweet expression of her pale, melancholy countenance.

"Daughter of mortality," said she, "what aileth thee? Why do thy tears trouble my fountain, and thy sighs and plaints disturb the quiet watches of the night?"

"I weep because of the faithlessness of man, and I bemoan my solitary and forsaken state."

"Take comfort; thy sorrows may yet have an end. Thou beholdest a Moorish princess, who, like thee, was unhappy in her love. A Christian knight, thy ancestor, won my heart, and would have borne me to his native land and to the bosom of his church. I was a convert in my heart, but I lacked courage equal to my faith, and lingered till too late. For this the evil genii are permitted to have power over me, and I remain enchanted in this tower until some pure Christian will deign to break the magic spell. Wilt thou undertake the task?"

"I will," replied the damsel, trembling.

"Come hither, then, and fear not; dip thy hand in the fountain, sprinkle the water over me, and baptize me after the manner of thy faith; so shall the enchantment be dispelled, and my troubled spirit shall have repose."

The damsel advanced with faltering steps, dipped her hand in the fountain, collected water in the palm, and sprinkled it over the pale face of the phantom.

The latter smiled with ineffable benignity. She dropped her silver lute at the feet of Jacinta, crossed her white arms upon her bosom, and melted from sight, so that it seemed merely as if a shower of dewdrops had fallen into the fountain.

Jacinta retired from the hall filled with awe and wonder. She scarcely closed her eyes that night; but when she awoke at daybreak out of a troubled slumber, the whole appeared to her like a distempered dream. On descending into the hall, however, the truth of the vision was established, for beside the fountain she beheld the silver lute glittering in the morning sunshine.

She hastened to her aunt, to relate all that had befallen

her, and called her to behold the lute as a testimonial of the reality of her story. If the good lady had any lingering doubts, they were removed when Jacinta touched the instrument, for she drew forth such ravishing tones as to thaw even the frigid bosom of the immaculate Fredegonda, that region of eternal winter, into a genial flow. Nothing but supernatural melody could have produced such an effect.

The extraordinary power of the lute became every day more and more apparent. The wayfarer passing by the tower was detained, and, as it were, spellbound in breathless ecstasy. The very birds gathered in the neighboring trees, and hushing their own strains, listened in charmed silence.

Rumor soon spread the news abroad. The inhabitants of Granada thronged to the Alhambra to catch a few notes of the transcendent music that floated about the Tower of Las Infantas.

The lovely little minstrel was at length drawn forth from her retreat. The rich and powerful of the land contended who should entertain and do honor to her; or rather, who should secure the charms of her lute to draw fashionable throngs to their saloons. Wherever she went her vigilant aunt kept a dragon watch at her elbow, awing the throngs of impassioned admirers who hung in raptures on her strains. The report of her wonderful powers spread from city to city. Malaga, Seville, Cordova, all became successively mad on the theme; nothing was talked of throughout Andalusia but the beautiful minstrel of the Alhambra. How could it be otherwise among a people so musical and gallant as the

Andalusians, when the lute was magical in its powers, and the minstrel inspired by love!

While all Andalusia was thus music mad, a different mood prevailed at the court of Spain. Philip V, as is well known, was a miserable hypochondriac, and subject to all kinds of fancies. Sometimes he would keep to his bed for weeks together, groaning under imaginary complaints. At other times he would insist upon abdicating his throne, to the great annoyance of his royal spouse, who had a strong relish for the splendors of a court and the glories of a crown, and guided the sceptre of her imbecile lord with an expert and steady hand.

Nothing was found to be so efficacious in dispelling the royal megrims as the power of music; the queen took care, therefore, to have the best performers, both vocal and instrumental, at hand, and retained the famous Italian singer Farinelli about the court as a kind of royal physician.

At the moment we treat of, however, a freak had come over the mind of this sapient and illustrious Bourbon that surpassed all former vagaries. After a long spell of imaginary illness, which set all the strains of Farinelli and the consultations of a whole orchestra of court fiddlers at defiance, the monarch fairly, in idea, gave up the ghost, and considered himself absolutely dead.

This would have been harmless enough, and even convenient both to his queen and courtiers, had he been content to remain in the quietude befitting a dead man; but to their annoyance he insisted upon having the funeral ceremonies performed over him, and, to their inexpressible perplexity, began to grow impatient, and to revile bitterly at them for negligence and disrespect, in leaving him unburied. What was to be done? To disobey the king's positive commands was monstrous in the eyes of the obsequious courtiers of a punctilious court—but to obey him, and bury him alive, would be downright regicide!

In the midst of this fearful dilemma a rumor reached the court of the female minstrel who was turning the brains of all Andalusia. The queen despatched missions in all haste to summon her to St. Ildefonso, where the court at that time resided.

Within a few days, as the queen with her maids of honor was walking in those stately gardens, intended, with their avenues and terraces and fountains, to eclipse the glories of Versailles, the far-famed minstrel was conducted into her presence. The imperial Elizabetta gazed with surprise at the youthful and unpretending appearance of the little being that had set the world madding. She was in her picturesque Andalusian dress, her silver lute in hand, and stood with modest and downcast eyes, but with a simplicity and fresh-ness of beauty that still bespoke her "the Rose of the Alhambra."

As usual she was accompanied by the ever-vigilant Fredegonda, who gave the whole history of her parentage and descent to the inquiring queen. If the stately Elizabetta had been interested by the appearance of Jacinta, she was still more pleased when she learnt that she was of a meritorious though impoverished line, and that her father had bravely fallen in the service of the crown. "If thy powers equal thy renown," said she, "and thou canst cast forth this evil spirit that possesses thy sovereign, thy fortunes shall henceforth be my care, and honors and wealth attend thee."

Impatient to make trial of her skill, she led the way at once to the apartment of the moody monarch.

Jacinta followed with downcast eyes through files of guards and crowds of courtiers. They arrived at length at a great chamber hung with black. The windows were closed to exclude the light of day; a number of yellow wax tapers in silver sconces diffused a lugubrious light, and dimly revealed the figures of mutes in mourning dresses, and courtiers who glided about with noiseless step and woebegone visage. In the midst of a funeral bed or bier, his hands folded on his breast, and the top of his nose just visible, lay extended this would-be-buried monarch.

The queen entered the chamber in silence, and pointing to a foot-stool in an obscure corner, beckoned to Jacinta to sit down and commence.

At first she touched her lute with a faltering hand, but gathering confidence and animation as she proceeded, drew forth such soft aërial harmony, that all present could scarce believe it mortal. As to the monarch, who had already considered himself in the world of spirits, he set it down for some angelic melody or the music of the spheres. By degrees the theme was varied, and the voice of the minstrel accompanied the instrument. She poured forth one of the legendary ballads treating of the ancient glories of the Alhambra and the achievements of the Moors. Her whole soul entered into the theme, for with the recollections of the Alhambra was associated the story of her love. The funeral-chamber resounded with the animating strain. It entered into the gloomy heart of the monarch. He raised his head and gazed around: he sat up on his couch, his eye began to kindle—at length, leaping upon the floor, he called for sword and buckler.

The triumph of music, or rather of the enchanted lute, was complete; the demon of melancholy was cast forth; and, as it were, a dead man brought to life. The windows of the apartment were thrown open; the glorious effulgence of Spanish sunshine burst into the late lugubrious chamber; all eyes sought the lovely enchantress, but the lute had fallen from her hand, she had sunk upon the earth, and the next moment was clasped to the bosom of Ruyz de Alarcon.

The nuptials of the happy couple were celebrated soon afterwards with great splendor, and the Rose of the Alhambra became the ornament and delight of the court. "But hold—not so fast"—I hear the reader exclaim; "this is jumping to the end of a story at a furious rate! First let us know how Ruyz de Alarcon managed to account to Jacinta for his long neglect?" Nothing more easy; the venerable, time-honored excuse, the opposition to his wishes by a proud, pragmatical old father; besides, young people who really like one another soon come to an amicable under-standing, and bury all past grievances when once they meet.

But how was the proud, pragmatical old father reconciled to the match?

Oh! as to that, his scruples were easily overcome by a word or two from the queen; especially as dignities and rewards were showered upon the blooming favorite of royalty. Besides, the lute of Jacinta, you know, possessed a magic power, and could control the most stubborn head and hardest breast.

And what came of the enchanted lute?

Oh, that is the most curious matter of all, and plainly proves the truth of the whole story. That lute remained for some time in the family, but was purloined and carried off, as was supposed, by the great singer Farinelli, in pure jealousy. At his death it passed into other hands in Italy, who were ignorant of its mystic powers, and melting down the silver, transferred the strings to an old Cremona fiddle. The strings still retain something of their magic virtues. A word in the reader's ear, but let it go no further: that fiddle is now bewitching the whole world,—it is the fiddle of Paganini!

From The Alhambra

Legend of the Two Discreet Statues

There lived once in a waste apartment of the Alhambra a merry little fellow, named Lope Sanchez, who worked in the gardens, and was as brisk and as blithe as a grasshopper, singing all day long. He was the life and soul of the fortress; when his work was over, he would sit on one of the stone benches of the esplanade, strum his guitar, and sing long ditties about the Cid, and Barnardo del Carpio, and Fernando del Pulgar, and other Spanish heroes, for the amusement of the old soldiers of the fortress; or would strike up a merrier tune, and set the girls dancing *boleros* and *fandangos*.

Like most little men, Lope Sanchez had a strapping buxom dame for a wife, who could almost have put him in her pocket; but he lacked the usual poor man's lot—instead of ten children he had but one. This was a little black-eyed girl about twelve years of age, named Sanchica, who was as merry as himself, and the delight of his heart. She played about him as he worked in the gardens, danced to his guitar as he sat in the shade, and ran as wild as a young fawn about the groves and alleys and ruined halls of the Alhambra.

It was now the eve of the blessed St. John, and the holiday-loving gossips of the Alhambra, men, women, and children, went up at night to the Mountain of the Sun, which rises above the Generalife, to keep their midsummer vigil on its level summit. It was a bright moonlight night, and all the mountains were gray and silvery, and the city, with its domes and spires, lay in shadows below, and the Vega was like a fairy land, with haunted streams gleaming among its dusky groves. On the highest part of the mountain they lit up a bonfire, according to an old custom of the country handed down from the Moors. The inhabitants of the surrounding country were keeping a similar vigil, and bonfires, here and there in the Vega, and along the folds of the mountains, blazed up palely in the moonlight.

The evening was gayly passed in dancing to the guitar of Lope Sanchez, who was never so joyous as when on a holiday revel of the kind. While the dance was going on, the little Sanchica with some of her playmates sported among the ruins of an old Moorish fort that crowns the mountain, when, in gathering pebbles in the fosse, she found a small hand curiously carved of jet, the fingers closed, and the thumb firmly clasped upon them. Overjoyed with her good fortune, she ran to her mother with her prize. It immediately became a subject of sage speculation, and was eyed by some with superstitious distrust. "Throw it away," said one; "it's Moorish,—depend upon it, there's mischief and witchcraft in it," "By no means," said another; "you may sell it for something to the jewellers of the Zacatin." In the midst of this discussion an old tawny soldier drew near, who had served in Africa, and was as swarthy as a Moor. He examined the hand with a knowing look. "I have seen things of this kind," said he, "among the Moors of Barbary. It is a great virtue to guard against the evil eye, and all kinds of spells and enchantments. I give you joy, friend Lope, this bodes good luck to your child."

Upon hearing this, the wife of Lope Sanchez tied the little hand of jet to a ribbon, and hung it round the neck of her daughter.

The sight of this talisman called up all the favorite superstitions about the Moors. The dance was neglected, and they sat in groups on the ground, telling old legendary tales handed down from their ancestors. Some of their stories turned upon the wonders of the very mountain upon which they were seated, which is a famous hobgoblin region. One ancient crone gave a long account of the subterranean palace in the bowels of that mountain where Boabdil and all his Moslem court are said to remain enchanted. "Among yonder ruins," said she, pointing to some crumbling walls and mounds of earth on a distant part of the mountain, "there is a deep black pit that goes down, down into the very heart of the mountain. For all the money in Granada I would not look down into it. Once upon a time a poor man of the Alhambra, who tended goats upon this mountain, scrambled down into that pit after a kid that had fallen in. He came out again all wild and staring, and told such things of what he had seen that every one thought his brain was turned. He raved for a day or two about the hobgoblin Moors that had pursued him in the cavern, and could hardly be persuaded to drive his goats up again to the mountain. He did so at last, but, poor man, he never came down again. The neighbors found his goats browsing about the Moorish ruins, and his hat and mantle lying near the mouth of the pit, but he was never more heard of."

The little Sanchica listened with breathless attention to his story. She was of a curious nature, and felt immediately a great hankering to peep into this dangerous pit. Stealing away from her companions, she sought the distant ruins, and, after groping for some time among them, came to a small hollow, or basin, near the brow of the mountain, where it swept steeply down into the valley of the Darro. In the centre of this basin yawned the mouth of the pit. Sanchica ventured to the verge, and peeped in. All was as black as pitch, and gave an idea of immeasurable depth. Her blood ran cold; she drew back, then peeped in again, then would have run away, then took another peep,—the very horror of the thing was delightful to her. At length she rolled a large stone, and pushed it over the brink. For some time it fell in silence; then struck some rocky projection with a violent crash; then rebounded from side to side, rumbling and tumbling, with a noise like thunder; then made a final splash into water, far below,—and all was again silent.

The silence, however, did not long continue. It seemed as if something had been awakened within this dreary abyss. A murmuring sound gradually rose out of the pit like the hum and buzz of a beehive. It grew louder and louder, there was the confusion of voices as of a distant multitude, together with the faint din of arms, clash of cymbals and clangor of trumpets, as if some army were marshalling for battle in the very bowels of the mountain.

The child drew off with silent awe, and hastened back to the place where she had left her parents and their companions. All were gone. The bonfire was expiring, and its last wreath of smoke curling up in the moonshine. The distant fires that had blazed along the mountains and in the Vega were all extinguished, and everything seemed to have sunk to repose. Sanchica called her parents and some of her companions by name, but received no reply. She ran down the side of the mountain, and by the gardens of the Generalife, until she arrived in the alley of trees leading to the Alhambra, when she seated herself on a bench of a woody recess, to recover breath. The bell from the watchtower of the Alhambra tolled midnight. There was a deep tranquility as if all nature slept; excepting the low tinkling sound of an unseen stream that ran under the covert of the bushes. The breathing sweetness of the atmosphere was lulling her to sleep, when her eye was caught by something glittering at a distance, and to her surprise she beheld a long cavalcade of Moorish warriors pouring down the mountain side and along the leafy avenues. Some were armed with lances and shields; others, with scimitars and battle-axes, and with polished cuirasses that flashed in the moonbeams. Their horses pranced proudly and champed upon their bits, but their tramp caused no more sound than if they had been shod with felt, and the riders were all as pale as death. Among them rode a beautiful lady, with a crowned head and long golden locks entwined with pearls. The housings of her palfrey were of crimson velvet embroidered with gold, and swept the earth; but she rode all disconsolate, with eyes ever fixed upon the ground.

Then succeeded a train of courtiers magnificently arrayed in robes and turbans of divers colors, and amidst them, on a cream-colored charger, rode King Boabdil el Chico, in a royal mantle covered with jewels, and a crown sparkling with diamonds. The little Sanchica knew him by his yellow beard, and his resemblance to his portrait, which she had often seen in the picture-gallery of the Generalife. She gazed in wonder and admiration at this royal pageant, as it passed glistening among the trees; but though she knew these monarchs and courtiers and warriors, so pale and silent, were out of the common course of nature, and things of magic and enchantment, yet she looked on with a bold heart, such courage did she derive from the mystic talisman of the hand, which was suspended about her neck.

The cavalcade having passed by, she rose and followed. It continued on to the great Gate of Justice, which stood wide open; the old invalid sentinels on duty lay on the stone benches of the barbican, buried in profound and apparently charmed sleep, and the phantom pageant swept noiselessly by them with flaunting banner and triumphant state. Sanchica would have followed; but to her surprise she beheld an opening in the earth, within the barbican, leading down beneath the foundations of the tower. She entered for a little distance, and was encouraged to proceed by finding steps rudely hewn in the rock, and a vaulted passage here and there lit up by a silver lamp, which, while it gave light, diffused likewise a grateful fragrance. Venturing on, she came at last to a great hall, wrought out of the heart of the mountain, magnificently furnished in the Moorish style, and lighted up by silver and crystal lamps. Here, on an ottoman, sat an old man in Moorish dress, with a long white beard, nodding and dozing, with a staff in his hand, which seemed ever to be slipping from his grasp; while at a little distance sat a beautiful lady, in ancient Spanish dress, with a coronet all sparkling with diamonds, and her hair entwined with pearls, who was softly playing on a silver lyre. The little Sanchica now recollected a story she had heard among the old people of the Alhambra, concerning a Gothic princess confined in the centre of the mountains by an old Arabian magician, whom she kept bound up in magic sleep by the power of music.

The lady paused with surprise at seeing a mortal in that enchanted hall. "Is it the eve of the blessed St. John?" said she.

"It is," replied Sanchica.

"Then for one night the magic charm is suspended. Come hither, child, and fear not. I am a Christian like thyself, though bound here by enchantment. Touch my fetters with the talisman that hangs about thy neck, and for this night I shall be free."

So saying she opened her robes and displayed a broad golden band round her waist, and a golden chain that fastened her to the ground. The child hesitated not to apply the little hand of jet to the golden band, and immediately the chain fell to the earth. At the sound the old man woke and began to rub his eyes; but the lady ran her fingers over the chords of the lyre, and again he fell into a slumber and began to nod, and his staff to falter in his hand. "Now," said the lady, "touch his staff with the talismanic hand of jet." The child did so, and it fell from his grasp, and he sank in a deep sleep on the ottoman. The lady gently laid the silver lyre on the ottoman, leaning it against the head of the sleeping magician; then touching the chords until they vibrated in his ear, —"O potent spirit of harmony," said she, "continue thus to hold his senses in thraldom till the return of day. Now follow me, my child," continued she, "and thou shalt behold the Alhambra as it was in the days of its glory, for thou hast a magic talisman that reveals all enchantments." Sanchica followed the lady in silence. They passed up through the entrance of the cavern into the barbican of the Gate of Justice, and thence to the Plaza de los Algibes, or esplanade within the fortress.

This was all filled with Moorish soldiery, horse and foot, marshalled in squadrons, with banners displayed. There were royal guards also at the portal, and rows of African blacks, with drawn scimitars. No one spoke a word, and Sanchica passed on fearlessly after her conductor. Her astonishment increased on entering the royal palace, in which she had been reared. The broad moonshine lit up all the halls and courts and gardens almost as brightly as if it were day, but revealed a far different scene from that to which she was accustomed. The walls of the apartments were no longer stained and rent by time. Instead of cobwebs, they were now hung with rich silks of Damascus, and the gildings and arabesque paintings were restored to their original brilliancy and freshness. The halls, no longer naked and unfurnished, were set out with divans and ottomans of the rarest stuffs, embroidered with pearls and studded with precious gems, and all the fountains in the courts and gardens were playing.

The kitchens were again in full operation. Cooks were busy preparing shadowy dishes, and roasting and boiling the phantoms of pullets and partridges; servants were hurrying to and fro with silver dishes heaped up with dainties, and arranging a delicious banquet. The Court of Lions was thronged with guards, and courtiers, and *alfaquis*, as in the old times of the Moors; and at the upper end, in the saloon of judgment, sat Boabdil on his throne, surrounded by his court, and swaying a shadowy sceptre for the night. Notwithstanding all this throng and seeming bustle, not a voice nor a footstep was to be heard; nothing interrupted the midnight silence but the splashing of the fountains. The little Sanchica followed her conductress in mute amazement about the palace, until they came to a portal opening to the vaulted passages beneath the great tower of Comares. On each side of the portal sat the figure of a nymph, wrought out of alabaster. Their heads were turned aside, and their regards fixed upon the same spot within the vault. The enchanted lady paused, and beckoned the child to her. "Here," said she, "is a great secret, which I will reveal to thee in reward for thy faith and courage. These discreet statues watch over a treasure, hidden in old times by a Moorish king. Tell thy father to search the spot on which their eyes are fixed, and he will find what will make him richer than any man in Granada. Thy innocent hands alone, however, gifted as thou art also with the talisman, can remove the treasure. Bid thy father use it discreetly, and devote a part of it to the performance of daily masses for my deliverance from this unholy enchantment."

When the lady had spoken these words, she led the child onward to the little garden of Lindaraxa, which is hard by the vault of the statues. The moon trembled upon the waters of the solitary fountain in the centre of the garden, and shed a tender light upon the orange and citron trees. The beautiful lady plucked a branch of myrtle and wreathed it round the head of the child. "Let this be a memento," said she, "of what I have revealed to thee, and a testimonial of its truth. My hour is come; I must return to the enchanted hall. Follow me not, lest evil befall thee. Farewell. Remember what I have said, and have masses performed for my deliverance." So saying, the lady entered a dark passage leading beneath the Tower of Comares, and was no longer seen.

The faint crowing of a cock was now heard from the cottages below the Alhambra, in the valley of the Darro, and a pale streak of light began to appear above the eastern mountains. A slight wind arose, there was a sound like the rustling of dry leaves through the courts and corridors, and door after door shut to with a jarring sound.

Sanchica returned to the scenes she had so lately beheld thronged with the shadowy multitude, but Boabdil and his phantom court were gone. The moon shone into empty halls and galleries stripped of their transient splendor, stained and dilapidated by time, and hung with cobwebs. The bat flitted about in the uncertain light, and the frog croaked from the fish-pond.

Sanchica now made the best of her way to a remote staircase that led up to the humble apartment occupied by her family. The door, as usual, was open, for Lope Sanchez was too poor to need bolt or bar. She crept quietly to her pallet, and, putting the myrtle wreath beneath her pillow, soon fell asleep.

In the morning she related all that had befallen her to her father. Lope Sanchez, however, treated the whole as a mere dream, and laughed at the child for her credulity. He went forth to his customary labors in the garden, but had not been there long when his little daughter came running to him, almost breathless. "Father! father!" cried she, "behold the myrtle wreath which the Moorish lady bound round my head!"

Lope Sanchez gazed with astonishment, for the stalk of the myrtle was of pure gold, and every leaf was a sparkling emerald! Being not much accustomed to precious stones, he was ignorant of the real value of the wreath, but he saw enough to convince him that it was something more substantial than the stuff of which dreams are generally made, and that at any rate the child had dreamt to some purpose. His first care was to enjoin the most absolute secrecy upon his daughter. In this respect, however, he was secure, for she had discretion far beyond her years or sex. He then repaired to the vault, where stood the statues of the two alabaster nymphs. He remarked that their heads were turned from the portal, and that the regards of each were fixed upon the same point in the interior of the building. Lope Sanchez could not but admire this most discreet contrivance for guarding a secret. He drew a line from the eyes of the statues to the point of regard, made a private mark on the wall, and then retired.

All day, however, the mind of Lope Sanchez was distracted with a thousand cares. He could not help hovering within distant view of the two statues, and became nervous from the dread that the golden secret might be discovered. Every footstep that approached the place made him tremble. He would have given anything could he but have turned the heads of the statues, forgetting that they had looked precisely in the same direction for some hundreds of years, without any person being the wiser.

"A plague upon them," he would say to himself, "they'll betray all; did ever mortal hear of such a mode of guarding a secret?" Then on hearing any one advance, he would steal off, as thought his very lurking near the place would awaken suspicion. Then he would return cautiously, and peep from a distance to see if everything was secure, but the sight of the statues would again call forth his indignation. "Ay, there they stand," would he say, "always looking and looking, and looking, just where they should not. Confound them! they are just like all their sex; if they have not tongues to tattle with, they'll be sure to do it with their eyes."

At length, to his relief, the long anxious day drew to a close. The sound of footsteps was no longer heard in the echoing halls of the Alhambra; the last stranger passed the threshold, the great portal was barred and bolted, and the bat and the frog and the hooting owl gradually resumed their nightly vocations in the deserted palace.

Lope Sanchez waited, however, until the night was far advanced before he ventured with his little daughter to the hall of the two nymphs. He found them looking as knowingly and mysteriously as ever at the secret place of deposit. "By your leave, gentle ladies," thought Lope Sanchez, as he passed between them, "I will relieve you from this charge that must have set so heavy in your minds for the last two or three centuries." He accordingly went to work at the part of the wall which he had marked, and in a little while laid open a concealed recess, in which stood two great jars of porcelain. He attempted to draw them forth, but they were immovable, until touched by the innocent hand of his little daughter. With her aid he dislodged them from their niche, and found, to his great joy, that they were filled with pieces of Moorish gold, mingled with jewels and precious stones. Before daylight he managed to convey them to his chamber, and left the two guardian statues with their eyes still fixed on the vacant wall.

Lope Sanchez had thus on a sudden become a rich man; but riches, as usual, brought a world of cares to which he had hitherto been a stranger. How was he to convey away his wealth with safety? How was he even to enter upon the enjoyment of it without awakening suspicion? Now, too, for the first time in his life the dread of robbers entered into his mind. He looked with terror at the insecurity of his habitation, and went to work to barricade the doors and windows; yet after all his precautions he could not sleep soundly. His usual gayety was at an end, he had no longer a joke or a song for his neighbors, and, in short, became the most miserable animal in the Alhambra. His old comrades remarked this alteration, pitied him heartily, and began to desert him; thinking he must be falling into want, and in danger of looking to them for assistance. Little did they suspect that his only calamity was riches.

The wife of Lope Sanchez shared his anxiety, but then she had ghostly comfort. We ought before this to have mentioned that Lope being rather a light inconsiderate little man, his wife was accustomed, in all grave matters, to seek the counsel and ministry of her confessor Fray Simon, a sturdy, broad-shouldered, blue-bearded, bullet-headed friar to the neighboring convent of San Francisco, who was in fact the spiritual comforter of half the good wives of the neighborhood. He was, moreover, in great esteem among divers sisterhoods of nuns; who requited him for his ghostly services by frequent presents of those little dainties and knick-knacks manufactured in convents, such as delicate confections, sweet biscuits, and bottles of spiced cordials, found to be marvellous restoratives after fasts and vigils.

Fray Simon thrived in the exercise of his functions. His

oily skin glistened in the sunshine as he toiled up the hill of the Alhambra on a sultry day. Yet notwithstanding his sleek condition, the knotted rope round his waist showed the austerity of his self-discipline; the multitude doffed their caps to him as a mirror of piety, and even the dogs scented the odor of sanctity that exhaled from his garments, and howled from their kennels as he passed.

Such was Fray Simon, the spiritual counsellor of the comely wife of Lope Sanchez; and as the father confessor is the domestic confidant of women in humble life in Spain, he was soon acquainted, in great secrecy, with the story of the hidden treasure.

The friar opened his eyes and mouth, and crossed himself a dozen times at the news. After a moment's pause, "Daughter of my soul!" said he, "know that thy husband has committed a double sin—a sin against both state and church! The treasure he hath thus seized upon for himself, being found in the royal domains, belongs of course to the crown; but being infidel wealth, rescued as it were from the very fangs of Satan, should be devoted to the church. Still, however, the matter may be accommodated. Bring hither thy myrtle wreath."

When the good father beheld it, his eyes twinkled more than ever with admiration of the size and beauty of the emeralds. "This," said he, "being the first-fruits of this discovery, should be dedicated to pious purposes. I will hang it up as a votive offering before the image of San Francisco in our chapel, and will earnestly pray to him, this very night, that your husband be permitted to remain in quiet possession of your wealth."

The good dame was delighted to make her peace with heaven at so cheap a rate, and the friar, putting the wreath under his mantle, departed with saintly steps toward his convent.

When Lope Sanchez came home, his wife told him what had passed. He was excessively provoked, for he lacked his wife's devotion, and had for some time groaned in secret at the domestic visitations of the friar. "Woman," said he, "what hast thou done? thou hast put everything at hazard by thy tattling."

"What!" cried the good woman, "would you forbid my disburdening my conscience to my confessor?"

"No, wife! confess as many of your own sins as you please; but as to this money-digging, it is a sin of my own, and my conscience is very easy under the weight of it."

There was no use, however, in complaining; the secret was told, and, like water spilled on the sand, was not again to be gathered. Their only chance was that the friar would be discreet.

The next day, while Lope Sanchez was abroad, there was an humble knocking at the door, and Fray Simon entered with meek and demure countenance.

"Daughter," said he, "I have earnestly prayed to San Francisco, and he has heard my prayer. In the dead of the night the saint appeared to me in a dream, but with a frowning aspect. 'Why,' said he, 'dost thou pray to me to dispense with this treasure of the Gentiles, when thou seest the poverty of my chapel? Go to the house of Lope Sanchez, crave in my name a portion of the Moorish gold, to furnish two candlesticks for the main altar, and let him possess the residue in peace'."

When the good woman heard of this vision, she crossed herself with awe, and going to the secret place where Lope had hid the treasure, she filled the great leathern purse with pieces of Moorish gold, and gave it to the friar. The pious monk bestowed upon her, in return, benedictions enough, if paid by heaven, to enrich her race to the latest posterity; then slipping the purse in the sleeve of his habit, he folded his hands upon his breast, and departed with an air of humble thankfulness.

When Lope Sanchez heard of this second donation to the church, he had wellnigh lost his senses. "Unfortunate man," cried he, "what will become of me? I shall be robbed by piecemeal; I shall be ruined and brought to beggary!"

It was with the utmost difficulty that his wife could pacify him, by reminding him of the countless wealth that yet remained, and how considerate it was for San Francisco to rest contented with so small a portion.

Unluckily Fray Simon had a number of poor relations to be provided for, not to mention some half-dozen sturdy bullet-headed orphan children and destitute foundlings that he had taken under his care. He repeated his visits, therefore, from day to day, with solicitations on behalf of Saint Dominick, Saint Andrew, Saint James, until poor Lope was driven to despair, and found that unless he got out of the reach of this holy friar he should have to make peace-offerings to every saint in the calendar. He determined, therefore, to pack up his remaining wealth, beat a secret retreat in the night, and make off to another part of the kingdom.

Full of his project he bought a stout mule for the purpose, and tethered it in a gloomy vault underneath the tower of the seven floors; the very place whence the Belludo, or goblin horse, is said to issue forth at midnight, and scour the streets of Granada, pursued by a pack of hellhounds. Lope Sanchez had little faith in the story, but availed himself of the dread occasioned by it, knowing that no one would be likely to pry into the subterranean stable of the phantom steed. He sent off his family in the course of the day, with orders to wait for him at a distant village of the Vega. As the night advanced he conveyed his treasure to the vault under the tower, and having loaded his mule, he led it forth and cautiously descended the dusky avenue.

Honest Lope had taken his measures with the utmost secrecy, imparting them to no one but the faithful wife of his bosom. By some miraculous revelation, however, they became known to Fray Simon. The zealous friar beheld these infidel treasures on the point of slipping forever out of his grasp, and determined to have one more dash at them for the benefit of the church and San Francisco. Accordingly, when the bells had rung for animas and all the Alhambra was quiet, he stole out of his convent, and descending through the Gate of Justice, concealed himself among the thickets of roses and laurels that border the great avenue. Here he remained, counting the quarters of hours as they were sounded on the bell of the watch-tower, and listening to the dreary hooting of owls, and the distant barking of dogs from the gypsy caverns.

At length he heard the tramp of hoofs, and, through the gloom of the overshading trees, imperfectly beheld a steed descending the avenue. The sturdy friar chuckled at the idea of the knowing turn he was about to serve honest Lope.

Tucking up the skirts of his habit, and wriggling like a cat watching a mouse, he waited until his prey was directly before him, when darting forth from his leafy covert, and putting one hand on the shoulder and the other on the crupper, he made a vault that would not have disgraced the most experienced master of equitation, and alighted well-forked astride the steed. "Ah ha!" said the sturdy friar, "we shall now see who best understands the game." He had scarce uttered the words when the mule began to kick, and rear, and plunge, and then set off full speed down the hill. The friar attempted to check him, but in vain. He bounded from rock to rock, and bush to bush; the friar's habit was torn to ribbons and fluttered in the wind, his shaven poll received many a hard knock from the branches of the trees, and many a scratch from the brambles. To add to his terror and distress, he found a pack of seven hounds in full cry at his heels, and perceived, too late, that he was actually mounted upon the terrible Belludo!

Away then they went, according to the ancient phrase, "pull devil, pull friar," down the great avenue, across the Plaza Nueva, along the Zacatin, around the Vivarrambla— never did huntsman and hound make a more furious run, or more infernal uproar. In vain did the friar invoke every saint in the calendar, and the holy Virgin into the bargain; every time he mentioned a name of the kind it was like a fresh application of the spur, and made the Belludo bound as high as a house. Through the remainder of the night was the unlucky Fray Simon carried hither and thither, and whither he would not, until every bone in his body ached, and he suffered a loss of leather too grievous to be mentioned. At length the crowing of a cock gave the signal of returning day. At the sound the goblin steed wheeled about, and galloped back for his tower. Again he scoured the Vivarrambla, the Zacatin, the Plaza Nueva, and the Avenue of Fountains, the seven dogs yelling and barking and leaping up, and snapping at the heels of the terrified friar. The first streak of day had just appeared as they reached the tower; here the goblin steed kicked up his heels, sent the friar a summerset through the air, plunged into the dark vault followed by the infernal pack, and a profound silence succeeded to the late deafening clamor.

Was ever so diabolical a trick played off upon a holy friar? A peasant going to his labors at early dawn found the unfortunate Fray Simon lying under a fig-tree at the foot of the tower, but so bruised and bedevilled that he could neither speak nor move. He was conveyed with all care and tenderness to his cell, and the story went that he had been waylaid and maltreated by robbers. A day or two elapsed before he recovered the use of his limbs; he consoled himself, in the meantime, with the thoughts that though the mule with the treasure had escaped him, he had previously had some rare pickings at the infidel spoils. His first care on being able to use his limbs was to search beneath his pallet, where he had secreted the myrtle wreath and the leathern pouches of gold extracted from the piety of Dame Sanchez. What was his dismay at finding the wreath, in effect, but a withered branch of myrtle, and the leathern pouches filled with sand and gravel!

Fray Simon, with all his chagrin, had the discretion to hold his tongue, for to betray the secret might draw on him the ridicule of the public and the punishment of his superior. It was not until many years afterwards, on his death-bed, that he revealed to his confessor his nocturnal ride on the Belludo.

Nothing was heard of Lope Sanchez for a long time after his disappearance from the Alhambra. His memory was always cherished as that of a merry companion, though it was feared, from the care and melancholy observed in his conduct shortly before his mysterious departure, that poverty and distress had driven him to some extremity. Some years afterwards one of his old companions, and invalid soldier, being at Malaga, was knocked down and nearly run over by a coach and six. The carriage stopped; an old gentleman, magnificently dressed, with a bag-wig and sword, stepped out to assist the poor invalid. What was the astonishment of the latter to behold in this grand cavalier his old friend Lope Sanchez, who was actually celebrating the marriage of his daughter Sanchica with one of the first grandees in the land.

The carriage contained the bridal party. There was Dame Sanchez, now grown as round as a barrel, and dressed out with feathers and jewels, and necklaces of pearls, and necklaces of diamonds, and rings on every finger, altogether a finery of apparel that had not been seen since the days of Queen Sheba. The little Sanchica had now grown to be a woman, and for grace and beauty might have been mistaken for a duchess, if not a princess outright. The bridegroom sat beside her—rather a withered, spindle-shanked little man, but this only proved him to be of the true blue blood; a legitimate Spanish grandee being rarely above three cubits in stature. The match had been of the mother's making.

Riches had not spoiled the heart of honest Lope. He kept his old comrade with him for several days; feasted him like a king, took him to plays and bull-fights, and at length sent him away rejoicing, with a big bag of money for himself, and another to be distributed among his ancient messmates of the Alhambra.

Lope always gave out that a rich brother had died in America and left him heir to a copper mine; but the shrewd gossips of the Alhambra insist that his wealth was all derived from his having discovered the secret guarded by the two marble nymphs of the Alhambra. It is remarked that these very discreet statues continue, even unto the present day, with their eyes fixed most significantly on the same part of the wall; which leads many to suppose there is still some hidden treasure remaining there well worthy the attention of the enterprising traveller. Though others, and particularly all female visitors, regard them with great complacency as lasting monuments of the fact that women can keep a secret.

From The Alhambra

Spanish Romance

*J*n the latter part of my sojourn in the Alhambra, I made frequent descents into the Jesuits' Library of the University; and relished more and more the old Spanish chronicles, which I found there bound in parchment. I delight in those quaint histories which treat of the times when the Moslems maintained a foothold in the Peninsula. With all their bigotry and occasional intolerance, they are full of noble acts and generous sentiments, and have a high, spicy, Oriental flavor, not to be found in other records of the times, which were merely European. In fact, Spain, even at the present day, is a country apart; severed in history, habits, manners, and modes of thinking, from all the rest of Europe. It is a romantic country; but its romance has none of the sentimentality of modern European romance; it is chiefly derived from the brilliant regions of the East, and from the high-minded school of Saracenic chivalry.

The Arab invasion and conquest brought a higher civilization, and a nobler style of thinking, into Gothic Spain. The Arabs were a quick witted, sagacious, proud-spirited, and poetical people, and were imbued with Oriental science and literature. Wherever they established a seat of power, it became a rallying-place for the learned and ingenious; and they softened and refined the people whom they conquered. By degrees, occupancy seemed to give them an hereditary right to their foothold in the land; they ceased to be looked upon as invaders, and were regarded as rival neighbors. The Peninsula, broken up into a variety of states, both Christian and Moslem, became, for centuries, a great campaigning-ground, where the art of war seemed to be the principal business of man, and was carried to the highest pitch of romantic chivalry. The original ground of hostility, a difference of faith, gradually lost its rancor. Neighboring states, of opposite creeds, were occasionally linked together in alliances, offensive and defensive; so that the cross and crescent were to be seen side by side, fighting against some common enemy. In times of peace, too, the noble youth of either faith resorted to the same cities, Christian or Moslem, to school themselves in military science. Even in the temporary truces of sanguinary wars, the warriors who had recently striven together in the deadly conflicts of the field, laid aside their animosity, met at tournaments, jousts, and other military festivities, and exchanged the courtesies of gentle and generous spirits. Thus the opposite races became frequently mingled together in peaceful intercourse, or if any rivalry took place, it was in those high courtesies and nobler acts, which bespeak the accomplished cavalier. Warriors, of opposite creeds, became ambitious of transcending each other in magnanimity as well as valor. Indeed, the chivalric virtues were refined upon to a degree sometimes fastidious and constrained, but at other times inexpressibly noble and affecting. The annals of the

times teem with illustrious instances of high-wrought courtesy, romantic generosity, lofty disinterestedness, and punctilious honor, that warm the very soul to read them. These
have furnished themes for national plays and poems, or have
been celebrated in those all pervading ballads, which are as
the life-breath of the people, and thus have continued to
exercise an influence on the national character, which centuries of vicissitude and decline have not been able to
destroy; so that, with all their faults, and they are many, the
Spaniards, even at the present day, are, on many points, the
most high-minded and proud-spirited people of Europe. It is
true, the romance of feeling derived from the sources I have
mentioned, has, like all other romance, its affectations and
extremes. It renders the Spaniard at times pompous and
grandiloquent; prone to carry the *pundonor*, or point of
honor, beyond the bounds of sober sense and sound morali-
ty; disposed, in the midst of poverty, to affect the *grande
caballero*, and to look down with sovereign disdain upon
"arts mechanical," and all the gainful pursuits of plebian life;
but this very inflation of spirit, while it fills his brain with
vapors, lifts him above a thousand meannesses; and though
it often keeps him in indigence, ever protects him from vul-
garity.

In the present day, when popular literature is running
into the low levels of life, and luxuriating on the vices and
follies of mankind; and when the universal pursuit of gain is
trampling down the early growth of poetic feeling, and wear-
ing out the verdure of the soul, I question whether it would

not be of service for the reader occasionally to turn to these records of prouder times and loftier modes of thinking; and to steep himself to the very lips in old Spanish romance.

With these preliminary suggestions, the fruit of a morning's reading and rumination in the old Jesuits' Library of the University, I will give him a legend in point, drawn forth from one of the venerable chronicles alluded to.

Legend of Don Munio Sancho de Hinojosa

In the cloisters of the ancient Benedictine convent of San Domingo, at Silos, in Castile, are the mouldering yet magnificent monuments of the once powerful and chivalrous family of Hinojosa. Among these reclines the marble figure of a knight, in complete armor, with the hands pressed together, as if in prayer. On one side of his tomb is sculptured in relief a band of Christian cavaliers, capturing a cavalcade of male and female Moors; on the other side, the same cavaliers are represented kneeling before an altar. The tomb, like most of the neighboring monuments, is almost in ruins, and the sculpture is nearly unintelligible, excepting to the keen eye of the antiquary. The story connected with the sepulchre, however, is still preserved in the old Spanish chronicles, and is to the following purport.

In old times, several hundred years ago, there was a noble Castilian cavalier, named Don Munio Sancho de Hinojosa, lord of a border castle, which had stood the brunt of many a Moorish foray. He had seventy horsemen as his household troops, all of the ancient Castilian proof; stark warriors, hard riders, and men of iron; with these he scoured the Moorish lands, and made his name terrible throughout the borders. His castle-hall was covered with banners, scimitars, and Moslem helms, the trophies of his prowess. Don Munio was, moreover, a keen huntsman; and rejoiced in hounds of all kinds, steeds for the chase, and hawks for the towering sport of falconry. When not engaged in warfare his delight was to beat up the neighboring forests; and scarcely ever did he ride forth without hound and horn, a boar-spear in his hand, or hawk upon his fist, and an attendant train of huntsmen.

His wife, Doña Maria Palacin, was of a gentle and timid nature, little fitted to be the spouse of so hardy and adventurous a knight; and many a tear did the poor lady shed, when he sallied forth upon his daring enterprises, and many a prayer did she offer up for his safety.

As this doughty cavalier was one day hunting, he stationed himself in a thicket, on the borders of a green glade of the forest, and dispersed his followers to rouse the game, and drive it toward his stand. He had not been here long, when a cavalcade of Moors, of both sexes, came prankling over the forest-lawn. They were unarmed, and magnificently dressed in robes of tissue and embroidery, rich shawls of India, bracelets and anklets of gold, and jewels that sparkled in the sun.

At the head of this gay cavalcade rode a youthful cavalier, superior to the rest in dignity and loftiness of demeanor, and in splendor of attire; beside him was a damsel, whose veil, blown aside by the breeze, displayed a face of surpassing beauty, and eyes cast down in maiden modesty, yet beaming with tenderness and joy.

Don Munio thanked his stars for sending him such a prize, and exulted at the thought of bearing home to his wife the glittering spoils of these infidels. Putting his hunting-horn to his lips, he gave a blast that wrung through the forest. His huntsmen came running from all quarters, and the astonished Moors were surrounded and made captives.

The beautiful Moor wrung her hands in despair, and her female attendants uttered the most piercing cries. The young Moorish cavalier alone retained self-possession. He inquired the name of the Christian knight who commanded this troop of horsemen. When told that it was Don Munio Sancho de Hinojosa, his countenance lighted up. Approaching that cavalier, and kissing his hand, "Don Munio Sancho," said he, "I have heard of your fame as a true and valiant knight, terrible in arms, but schooled in the noble virtues of chivalry. Such do I trust to find you. In me you behold Abadil, son of a Moorish Alcalde. I am on the way to celebrate my nuptials with this lady; chance has thrown us in your power, but I confide in your magnanimity. Take all our treasure and jewels; demand what ransom you think proper for our persons, but suffer us not to be insulted nor dishonored."

When the good knight heard this appeal, and beheld the beauty of the youthful pair, his heart was touched with tenderness and courtesy. "God forbid," said he, "that I should disturb such happy nuptials. My prisoners in troth shall ye be, for fifteen days, and immured within my castle, where I claim, as conqueror, the right of celebrating your espousals."

So saying, he despatched one of his fleetest horsemen in advance, to notify Doña Maria Palacin of the coming of this bridal party; while he and his huntsmen escorted the cavalcade, not as captors, but as a guard of honor. As they drew near to the castle, the banners were hung out, and the trumpets sounded from the battlements; and on their nearer approach, the drawbridge was lowered, and Doña Maria came forth to meet them, attended by her ladies and knights, her pages and her minstrels. She took the young bride, Allifra, in her arms, kissed her with the tenderness of a sister, and conducted her into the castle. In the meantime, Don Munio sent forth missives in every direction, and had viands and dainties of all kinds collected from the country round; and the wedding of the Moorish lovers was celebrated with all possible state and festivity. For fifteen days the castle was given up to joy and revelry. There were tiltings and jousts at the ring, and bull-fights, and banquets, and dances to the sound of minstrelsy. When the fifteen days were at an end, he made the bride and bridegroom magnificent presents, and conducted them and their attendants safely beyond the borders. Such, in old times, were the courtesy and generosity of a Spanish cavalier.

Several years after this event, the king of Castile summoned his nobles to assist him in a campaign against the Moors. Don Munio Sancho was among the first to answer to the call, with seventy horsemen, all stanch and well-tried warriors. His wife, Doña Maria, hung about his neck. "Alas, my lord!" exclaimed she, "how often wilt thou tempt thy fate, and when will thy thirst for glory be appeased!"

"One battle more," replied Don Munio, "one battle more, for the honor of Castile, and I here make a vow that, when this is over, I will lay by my sword, and repair with my cavaliers in pilgrimage to the sepulchre of our Lord at Jerusalem." The cavaliers all joined with him in the vow, and Doña Maria felt in some degree soothed in spirit; still, she saw with a heavy heart the departure of her husband, and watched his banner with wistful eyes, until it disappeared among the trees of the forest. The king of Castile led his army to the plains of Salmanara, where they encountered the Moorish host, near to Ucles. The battle was long and bloody; the Christians repeatedly wavered and were as often rallied by the energy of their commanders. Don Munio was covered with wounds, but refused to leave the field. The Christians at length gave way, and the king was hardly pressed, and in danger of being captured.

Don Munio called upon his cavaliers to follow him to the rescue. "Now is the time," cried he, "to prove your loyalty. Fall to, like brave men! We fight for the true faith, and if we lose our lives here, we gain a better life hereafter."

Rushing with his men between the king and his pursuers, they checked the latter in their career, and gave time for their monarch to escape; but they fell victims to their loyalty. They all fought to the last gasp. Don Munio was singled out by a powerful Moorish knight, but having been wounded in the right arm, he fought to disadvantage, and was slain. The battle being over, the Moor paused to possess himself of the spoils of this redoubtable Christian warrior. When he unlaced the helmet, however, and beheld the countenance of Don Munio, he gave a great cry and smote his breast. "Woe is me!" cried he, "I have slain my benefactor! The flower of knightly virtue! the most magnanimous of cavaliers!"

While the battle had been raging on the plain of Salmanara, Doña Maria Palacin remained in her castle, a prey to the keenest anxiety. Her eyes were ever fixed on the road that led from the country of the Moors, and often she asked the watchman of the tower, "What seest thou?"

One evening, at the shadowy hour of twilight, the warden sounded his horn. "I see," cried he, "a numerous train winding up the valley. There are mingled Moors and Christians. The banner of my lord is in the advance. Joyful tidings!" exclaimed the old seneschal; "my lord returns in triumph, and brings captives!" Then the castle courts rang with shouts of joy; and the standard was displayed, and the trumpets were sounded, and the drawbridge was lowered, and Doña Maria went forth with her ladies, and her knights, and her pages, and her minstrels, to welcome her lord from the wars. But as the train drew nigh, she beheld a sumptuous bier, covered with black velvet, and on it lay a warrior, as if taking his repose: he lay in his armor, with his helmet on his head, and his sword in his hand, as one who had never been conquered, and around the bier were the escutcheons of the house of Hinojosa.

A number of Moorish cavaliers attended the bier, with emblems of mourning, and with dejected countenances; and their leader cast himself at the feet of Doña Maria, and hid his face in his hands. She beheld in him the gallant Abadil, whom she had once welcomed with his bride to her castle; but who now came with the body of her lord, whom he had unknowingly slain in battle!

The sepulchre erected in the cloisters of the convent of San Domingo was achieved at the expense of the Moor Abadil, as a feeble testimony of his grief for the death of the good knight Don Munio, and his reverence for his memory. The tender and faithful Doña Maria soon followed her lord to the tomb. On one of the stones of a small arch, beside his sepulchre, is the following simple inscription: *"Hic jacet Maria Palacin, uxor Munonis Sancij De Finojosa"*—Here lies Maria Palacin, wife of Munio Sancho de Hinojosa.

The legend of Don Munio Sancho does not conclude with his death. On the same day on which the battle took place on the plain of Salmanara, a chaplain of the Holy Temple at Jerusalem, while standing at the outer gate, beheld a train of Christian cavaliers advancing, as if in pilgrimage. The chaplain was a native of Spain, and as the pilgrims approached, he knew the foremost to be Don Munio Sancho de Hinojosa, with whom he had been well acquainted in former times. Hastening to the patriarch, he told him of the honorable rank of the pilgrims at the gate. The patriarch, therefore, went forth with a grand procession of priests and monks, and received the pilgrims with all due honor. There were seventy cavaliers beside their leader,—all stark and lofty warriors. They carried their helmets in their hands, and their faces were deadly pale. They greeted no one, nor looked either to the right or to the left, but entered the chapel, and kneeling before the sepulchre of our Saviour, performed their orisons in silence. When they had concluded, they rose as if to depart, and the patriarch and his attendants advanced to speak to them, but they were no more to be seen. Every one marvelled what could be the meaning of this prodigy. The patriarch carefully noted down the day, and sent to Castile to learn tidings of Don Munio Sancho de Hinojosa. He received for reply, that, on the very day specified, that worthy knight, with seventy of his followers, had been slain in battle. These, therefore, must have been the blessed spirits of those Christian warriors, come to fulfil their vow of pilgrimage to the Holy Sepulchre at Jerusalem. Such was Castilian faith in the olden time, which kept its word, even beyond the grave.

If any one should doubt of the miraculous apparition of these phantom knights, let him consult the "History of the Kings of Castile and Leon," by the learned and pious Fray Prudencio de Sandoval, Bishop of Pamplona, where he will find it recorded in the "History of King Don Alonzo VI," on the hundred and second page. It is too precious a legend to be lightly abandoned to the doubter.

From The Alhambra

THE BEAUTIFUL
Illustrated Junior Library®
EDITIONS